ALL THE LONELY PEOPLE

The brand-new Rafferty and Llewellyn Mystery

When Detective Inspector Joseph Rafferty visits his local for a quick drink or three, he's looking to forget his troubles, not add to them. His personal life is in a state of great confusion. But, after a very public argument, a man is found dead (stabbed to death in the pub's car park) and a gloomy Rafferty gets out the breath freshener, and gets on the case, with the Super breathing down his neck.

ALL THE LONELY PEOPLE

A Rafferty & Llewellyn Crime Novel

Geraldine Evans

Severn House Large Print
London & New York

This first large print edition published 2012
in Great Britain and the USA by
SEVERN HOUSE PUBLISHERS LTD of
9-15 High Street, Sutton, Surrey, SM1 1DF.
First world regular print edition published 2009 by
Severn House Publishers Ltd., London and New York.

British Library Cataloguing in Publication Data

Evans, Geraldine.
    All the lonely people. -- (A Rafferty and Llewellyn
    mystery)
    1. Rafferty, Joseph (Fictitious character)--Fiction.
    2. Llewellyn, Sergeant (Fictitious character)--Fiction.
    3. Police--Great Britain--Fiction. 4. Detective and
    mystery stories. 5. Large type books.
    I. Title II. Series
    823.9'2-dc23

ISBN-13: 978-0-7278-9887-6

Severn House Publishers support The Forest Stewardship Council
[FSC], the leading international forest certification organisation. All
our titles that are printed on Greenpeace-approved FSC-certified paper
carry the FSC logo.

MIX
Paper from
responsible sources
FSC
www.fsc.org   FSC® C018575

Printed and bound in Great Britain by the
MPG Books Group, Bodmin, Cornwall.

George, my darling, this one's for you.
Thank you for all your care and kindness
over the last few years.

ONE

Detective Inspector Joseph Rafferty entered the saloon bar of The Railway Arms and looked around to see if there was anyone in that he knew. He couldn't see any familiar faces, but there was a good crowd in and he had to sidle his way through the throng to the bar. He recognized a few regulars as he passed and he said hello. Andy Strong, the landlord, was behind the counter and asked Rafferty if he wanted his usual.

Rafferty nodded. 'Please. The short usual rather than the long one.' He felt in need of a livener and he watched as Andy put a glass under the Jameson optic, pushed it up and measured out a double. Rafferty kept an eagle eye out, always wary of short measures – not that Andy was a landlord who had ever been cautioned for short-changing his customers – but you could never be sure.

'Not seen you in for a while, Joe, nor Abra for that matter,' Andy said as he put the glass on the bar and took Rafferty's money. 'You two had a falling out?'

'You could say that. At least, Abra's had a falling out with *me*.'

'What happened? You been playing away?' he asked over his shoulder as he rang up the money in the till before turning back and handing Rafferty his change. Andy was ex-army and tended to be straight to the point in his manner. It went with the epauletted shirt and short back and sides.

'No. Nothing like that. Abra thought I was trying to cheese-pare on the wedding arrangements. We had a big bust-up and now she's not talking to me.'

'So she decided to do without the groom, is that it?'

'Got it in one.' Morosely, he sipped his whiskey. A roar went up from the public bar. 'Noisy in here tonight.'

'Got a stag party in. They're getting more raucous by the minute. I'll have to turf them out if it carries on.'

Andy could handle himself. He kept fit and was a regular at the gym. He and Vivienne – Viv – his wife, kept a well-run pub and it was rare for the police to be called out to any kind of trouble. Another customer in the public bar claimed the landlord's attention and he left Rafferty to his lonely supping.

The news about the stag do made him maudlin, wondering when – if – he'd have a stag party of his own. It was one part of the wedding hullabaloo that he'd actually looked forward to, being free of the stiff, starchy speechifying and extortionate charging of so much of the rest of the marital rite of passage. Perhaps, given the circumstances, the nearest he'd get to a stag do was asking to be invited to join this one.

Abra, his fiancée, had proved intransigent after their row. If, that was, she was still his fiancée. All along, he'd expected her to see sense about being extravagant over their wedding, but it hadn't happened. And now look where they found themselves. Rafferty downed the rest of his Jameson's and ordered another from the barmaid. At least Abra hadn't given him the engagement ring back, which surprised him as she'd had plenty of time to do so. Where there was a ring there was hope, he told himself, though he was no longer so sure that this was true.

He sipped the second whiskey more slowly, conscious that he couldn't continue to drink his sorrows away as he'd been doing. But it had been three months now and Abra still wouldn't speak to him. He'd called round to her flat and rung her repeatedly, but she had refused to talk to him. He didn't know what else to do to get her back, though his police partner, Dafyd Llewellyn, Abra's cousin, had offered his services as a mediator. But for that to work Abra needed to agree to meet him.

It was his own fault, of course. He knew that. If he hadn't tried to keep their wedding costs within reason, he wouldn't be having this lonely drink while listening to some other soon-to-be groom celebrating his stag night.

They were getting even more raucous. Rafferty could hear them clearly through the wooden partition that separated the two main bars. They were now singing some rude rugby ditty. Out of the corner of his eye, Rafferty saw the landlord lift the bar counter and shout to them to tone it down a bit. It didn't seem to have any effect; the singing continued as loudly as before.

One of the regulars came over to talk to Rafferty and they exchanged football lore for the next five minutes, thrashing away at the winners and losers of the Premiership, but Rafferty's heart wasn't really in it and his football buddy wandered back to his other friends soon after, leaving Rafferty free to stare disconsolately around him.

The Railway Arms was a true piece of Victoriana, from its decorative plate glass mirror behind the bar, to the carved wood embellishing the booths. By some miracle, it had never been altered by the mad modernizers like several of the other historic pubs in the town. It was one of Rafferty's favourite watering holes and he often popped in after work for a quick one. It was on the way home and the service was always good, not like some of the town's other pubs where bored barmaids took their own sweet time to serve or even notice you. He was here much later than usual tonight as he had got tired of his own company in his flat. He'd just come in for the last knockings and would only stay till chucking out time. Just long enough to take the edge off his loneliness and enable him to sleep without bad dreams about Abra finding a rich man who was eager to marry her and who indulged her most extravagant marital excesses.

The booths – some four of them lined the walls of the saloon bar – had benches that were made of mahogany. Say one thing for the Victorians, they didn't stint – their backs were intricately carved with designs of the famous steam trains of the day: the Flying Scotsman, the Great Western, the Rocket and the Papyrus. The booth seats were crimson plush, recently redone. The curtains that had once screened each booth were long gone. In their place were small swing doors, about a third the length of the door-sized gap. They gave an illusion of privacy at sitting down head level.

Pictures of Elmhurst in the Victorian railway heyday lined the walls, full of uniformed railwaymen, from the stern-visaged stationmaster proudly displaying his pocket watch like a badge of office, to the young lad dogsbody with his pale face and spindly limbs. Other pictures showed carriages lined up to collect the gentry off the London train.

The whole pub was a peon of praise to a long-gone era and its glorious over-the-topness. The Victorians, when they believed in doing something, did it to the hilt and beyond. Theirs had been an age in British history that Rafferty strongly admired: tenacious, go-getting, ambitious. Sometimes, he thought it was an era he would have liked to have been part of. But then he remembered his family were Irish peasants on both sides. There would have been no proud brandishing of the flag across the Empire for him. He was more likely to die in agony of gangrene in some disgusting field hospital in the Crimea before Florence Nightingale – with her up-to-date ideas about hygiene – arrived.

The stag-night boys were getting louder, the rugby songs ruder. A couple of the women who had been sitting in one of the window seats got up and left in a marked manner muttering about drunken yobs. Rafferty grinned and walked across to claim one of their abandoned seats. The pub was busy and he was lucky to get it; he just beat a couple to the place.

The Railway Arms was the handiest pub for the station, of course, and some of the commuters came in from the trains and forgot to go home. It was a good-sized pub with two large bars and a small snug to the rear. It wasn't the oldest pub in Elmhurst, having been built when the railway was run through the town, but it was comfortable, with clean, well-kept toilets. As an ex-army man, Andy Strong was a stickler for brass and blanco.

It quietened down a bit. But then five minutes later, he heard shouting from the other bar. He was seated near the partition and could hear it clearly.

'What the bloody hell are *you* doing here? You weren't invited.'

'Free country, son. A free house, too. I can come in here if I choose.'

'Bloody old bastard. Why don't you sling your hook? I don't want you gatecrashing my stag do. Go home, why don't you. You're pissed.'

Rafferty waited for the argument to continue. Instead, they sidestepped the row and went straight for the fisticuffs. He heard the crunch of a fist connecting to flesh and bone and then the crash of falling chairs.

It seemed the landlord had had enough, for he bellowed loud enough to raise the dead, 'Right. That's it. Out, the lot of you. I've my other customers to consider.'

There were some more raucous shouts from Andy's boisterous customers, then the bar doors banged and the place quietened down considerably.

Rafferty returned to the study of his whiskey. He supposed he ought to go, too. Back to the empty flat. It wasn't a pleasing prospect and had become less pleasing the longer it had gone on. But if he stayed, he'd only have more to drink and would have to leave his car in the pub car park with all the trouble of fetching it in the morning.

He was just shrugging into his jacket, when he heard more shouting.

'Hey, Andy,' someone called to the landlord from the door of the public bar. 'One of your customers is curled up drunk in your yard. You'd better shift him and pour him into a taxi before someone runs over him.'

Muttering, Andy Strong raised the bar counter again and followed the customer out. He was back inside two minutes and came straight across to Rafferty. 'You're a copper,' he said. 'Trained up in first aid and so on. Only I've got a customer in the car park and I can't rouse him. Will you come and have a look?'

Rafferty sighed, finished his drink and followed the landlord out and round the side of the building to the car park. It was surprisingly quiet; they could have been outside a country pub, the night was so peaceful. It was surprising they could hear none of the noisy hubbub of the bar.

The weather was still mild though a slight breeze had blown up. It ruffled his hair, but it had no effect on Andy's grey regulation short back and sides, which was as disciplined as the rest of him and stayed put whatever the weather. There was a row of lights illuminating the part of the yard nearest the pub, but the darkness increased the further they got from the building, the cars' shadows stretching out lengthily and adding to the gloom of the yard.

The landlord threaded his way through the darkness with a sure and confident step. He rounded a couple of parked cars and pointed. 'There he is.'

Rafferty stared over Andy Strong's shoulder for several seconds, but the parked cars shadowed the spreadeagled body and he could make out little. 'Hang on,' he said. 'I'll get my torch from the car.' He hurried across to his vehicle and rummaged in the glove compartment for a little before his fingers found the hard surface of the torch. He was back in a couple of minutes. He edged past the landlord and shone the torch over the man on the ground. He had thought the sudden light would help to rouse the man from his stupor, but it had no effect. He knelt down and felt for a pulse.

'I've already done that,' Andy told him. 'I couldn't feel anything.'

Nor could Rafferty. He stood up again and played the torch slowly over the man's body, which he was beginning to suspect was actually a corpse. He was certain of it when he saw the slit in the man's jacket right between the shoulder blades and what looked like blood seeped around the edges of the slit. 'He's been knifed,' he said, the thought of his lonely flat receding and becoming more attractive as the possibility of reaching it vanished into the distance. He'd have to call the team out.

'Do you know his name?' Rafferty asked the landlord. 'His face is familiar, but I've only seen him in here a couple of times.'

Strong nodded. 'His name's Keith Sutherland. One of my regulars.' He paused, then added sombrely, 'Or he used to be.' He added with a degree of reluctance, 'He had a row with his son earlier.' He gave a quick glance at Rafferty. 'Do you think the son might have done this?'

'I don't know, Andy. Do you?'

Andy stood uncharacteristically indecisive

16

for several moments before shaking his head.

'That, I presume, was Keith Sutherland and his son I heard shouting the odds at one another in the public bar? The ones you chucked out of the pub together a few minutes before this man's body was found?'

Andy confirmed it.

The landlord had given him a lot to think about. It wasn't often he had such an easy murder suspect handed to him on a plate. He could get to like it. He pulled his mobile phone from his pocket and called the station to get the team mobilized. That done, he turned to Andy. 'I want you to lock the pub doors and keep the customers inside. I don't want anyone scuttling off until they've been questioned and given their names and addresses.' Though, he knew, in all likelihood their killer had already fled into the night. 'I'll have to stay with the body while you do that. I don't want to risk anyone interfering with the crime scene. Just tell your customers that someone's been killed in your yard and they'll have to stay till the police arrive. Don't tell them any more than that.'

'They won't like that.'

'Too bad. They'll just have to lump it.'

Andy stared at him for several seconds before he nodded again and marched purposefully back to the pub. Rafferty was left

17

alone with the corpse. He looked down at the body stretched out, with its face resting against the cold tarmac. He shivered and moved away a few yards, nearer to the pub lights.

It was eerie in the yard. The night seemed darker and more threatening now that the reassuring bulk of Andy Strong had gone. The wind had got up even more and whistled through the trees in the neighbouring gardens, blowing litter into the pub yard which Andy usually swept clean several times a day.

Rafferty pulled his jacket collar closer to his ears and angled his watch to the light to see how much time had passed and how soon he could expect the arrival of his police colleagues. But only five minutes had gone by. He sighed. It would be a while yet before he could expect company. While he waited, he spent the time noting down details of the vehicles in the yard and their registration numbers. Thus passed another five minutes and at the end of it, he saw the first flashing lights of a police car as it pulled up at the kerb; it was quickly followed by another.

Soon, the entire team was assembled. Rafferty had a quick word with them, explaining the situation, and left them to the well-ordered routine of securing the scene. He instructed two of the uniformed officers to return with him to the pub. He banged on the door and the landlord opened up and let him and the other two men in, locking the door again behind them as Rafferty instructed. Once back in the bar, he and the landlord were immediately surrounded by a crowd of belligerent, questioning customers. They became more belligerent when Rafferty announced that no one could go home yet. They grumbled even more when Andy Strong threw tea towels over the pumps, signalling that the evening's pleasure was at an end. Rafferty was pleased to see it. He'd have told him to do so if the landlord hadn't acted on his own initiative; he didn't want his potential witnesses any more befuddled than they were already.

Rafferty quickly divided the customers into two groups for initial questioning by the uniformed officers and then went back to the car park and the corpse. This time, he went out through the pub kitchen rather than have Andy do door duty again.

The body was still there unfortunately. Not a figment of his imagination then, he thought. Pity. It meant it would be a long night.

TWO

The pub customers were waiting in a raggedy line in front of the two uniformed officers to take their turns at giving their details and anything they recalled of the evening. The officers had commandeered a table apiece and were working methodically through the lines, taking names and addresses and any other relevant information. The customers still grumbled amongst themselves, but in lowered tones as if they were anxious about disturbing the corpse, which was still laid out in the pub's yard. In spite of their lowered tones, they were getting querulous. The information they gave was sparse enough. Rafferty stood and listened to some of the customers who had been in the public bar and they all said the same thing: that the dead man had entered the public bar from the door leading from the snug and accosted the stag party members. Certainly, no one admitted to going out to the car park during the latter part of the evening. But as Rafferty knew, anyone could have done so. People had been in and out of the bar since he entered the pub; going out for a cigarette since the ban on smoking in pubs came into force; going out to the toilets, which were situated at the entrance to the bars. He'd heard the door from the public bar bang a number of times. Any one of them could have taken him or herself round to the pub yard and waited their chance to stab Sutherland.

Naturally, all this information gathering took some time. There had been thirty customers in the pub at the time the body was discovered and another ten or so who had left the pub before then: they would also have to be questioned, of course. Rafferty had managed to get the names of most of them from the landlord. As for the others, he could only hope they came forward when news of the murder broke as the landlord only knew them by their first names or nicknames and didn't know where most of them lived.

'I'll need to speak to the man who found the body,' Rafferty told Andy Strong. He glanced round the bar and asked, 'Is he still here?'

'No,' Andy told him. 'He drove off after he called me outside.'

'Do you know his name and address?'

Andy nodded.

Rafferty got out his notebook and jotted down the details. He'd need to speak to the man as soon as possible. He might have noticed something and close questioning could jog his memory if it needed jogging. While he was at it, he also obtained the names of as many of the customers who had left the bar as Andy was able to tell him.

Rafferty missed Llewellyn. Dafyd was good at the routine stuff, but was away until tomorrow. Or rather – he glanced at his watch and saw it was 12.30 in the morning – later today now.

The bar was finally quiet. Almost all of the customers had been questioned and had left, leaving only two remaining. Rafferty propped himself up at the bar, an on-the-house whiskey in front of him. 'So, tell me about Keith Sutherland,' he invited the landlord. 'Why would anyone want to kill him?'

Andy Strong gave a shrug at Rafferty's question. He turned and poured himself a stiff brandy before he answered. 'Keith was the sort of bloke who rubbed others up the wrong way. He was always getting into arguments with people. He even had a shouting match with his son tonight, as I told you earlier.'

'That was him, was it?' Rafferty wanted to be sure on this point.

Andy Strong nodded, his silver hair glinting as it caught the lights above the bar. 'Ian Sutherland is getting married in a few weeks. That was his stag do I told you about earlier.'

'And from what I heard, the father wasn't invited.'

'That's right. He was dead set against the boy marrying Georgie, his fiancée. Thought she was a gold digger. After the son's inheritance.'

'Was the victim rich, then?'

'Not so's you'd notice. I never saw him flinging his money about in here, anyway, though I knew he had his own business.'

Rafferty nodded, interested to get another possible motive for the murder. Andy's information meant that Sutherland's son had two reasons to wish his father dead. 'I take it the dead man was married?'

'Yes.' The landlord kept busy polishing glasses while he spoke to Rafferty. He was as thorough in this as he was in everything else and already had an array of them lined up gleaming on the shelf. 'His wife's named Mary. There's a daughter, too, name of Susie. Ian and Susie are both in their twenties. Neither of the kids live at home. I think they left as soon as they could support themselves, in order to get away from their old man.'

'Can you let me have a list of those of your customers he'd had rows with?'

'Quicker to let you have a list of those he didn't row with.' He glanced at Rafferty and sighed. 'OK. I can try. Might be a long list.' Andy hung the tea towel he had used to polish the glasses on the pumps and went off to find a writing pad and a pen.

Dr Sam Dally arrived as the last customer was ushered out. 'Struck lucky, didn't you, Rafferty?' he said as he came up to the bar. 'Having a murder investigation set in a pub. Going to set up the incident room in the snug?'

'I wish. No. The incident room will be set up at the station. It's near enough to the scene.' The police station was only about a hundred yards up Station Road and over the crossroads.

'So what have we got?'

'A stabbing. Through the heart, by the look of it.'

'Where's the body?'

'In the car park.' Rafferty downed his drink in one swallow, nodded at Andy Strong who was busy writing his list and said, 'Come on, I'll show you.'

'I'll get into my protective gear first. I've got some stashed in the car.' Sam eyed Rafferty's jacket and trousers. 'Maybe you ought to do likewise?'

'Bit late for that.' But he followed Sam out to his car and took the protective gear Sam handed him and put it on before he led the pathologist to the scene.

The pub car park was a hub of activity. Arc lights had been set up and made the yard as light as day. The Scene of Crime team were busy doing a fingertip search, made easier now that nearly all the cars had left the yard. The previous darkness had been kinder to the corpse. And Rafferty. But now the body was starkly lit and the victim's skin looked waxy, the blood on the thin, light-coloured jacket more vivid.

Lance Edwards, the photographer, who had not long arrived, finished his work as they approached. He made way for Dally, who knelt by the body, eased down the trousers and started to take the rectal temperature.

But this last was scarcely necessary. According to the landlord, there had only been around ten minutes between him ordering Keith Sutherland from the bar and his body being found, something Rafferty could corroborate, as could the other customers who had witnessed it. Time of death was the easy part. Clearly, also, Sutherland had died where he had been found, as Dally soon confirmed from the hypostasis evidence.

'You hardly need me,' Dally complained as he finished his probing of the body and stood up. 'You could have left me in my comfortable bed with my comfortable lady.'

'And have you miss all the fun? I reckon if you ask nicely, the landlord will be able to find you a single malt to console you.'

Dally's half-moon glasses glinted under the arc lights. 'Now you're talking. One won't put me over the limit. Lead on, McDuff.'

Five minutes later, Rafferty and Sam Dally were seated companionably at the bar, two single malts in front of them.

'So what more can you tell me, Sam?' Rafferty asked as he appreciatively sipped his drink.

'One thrust through the heart, as you saw for yourself. Don't ask me any more till I've done the post-mortem as I shan't tell you.'

'Always the hard man.'

'So,' said Sam, changing the subject as he held his glass up to the light over the bar and sighed contentedly. 'What's the news on the Abra front?'

Rafferty pulled a face. 'Much the same as it was last time you asked. She's still not talking to me. I've got Dafyd to promise to try his hand at mediation. See if we can't patch things up.'

'It's a bad do when you have a big bust-up

before the wedding. Makes you wonder how many sparks'll be flying after.'

'If we ever get to after,' Rafferty muttered. He downed his malt and stood up. 'Now, suitably fortified, I have to go and break the news to the victim's family.'

Dally gave a mischievous smile and said, 'Makes me glad I only deal with dead people.'

The victim had been robbed of his wallet, but luckily, for purposes of identification confirmation, he had a gas bill in his pocket, so they had Sutherland's address, which Andy Strong had been unable to supply.

Rafferty rounded up Lizzie Green with Timothy Smales to drive them and headed for Sutherland's home through Elmhurst's quiet streets. Fortunately it was a Thursday with tomorrow a working day, so the majority of the revellers that the weekend would spawn were home in bed.

The Sutherlands' house was in darkness, of course. Mrs Sutherland must have long since gone to bed. Rafferty didn't relish the necessity of waking her up and breaking the news, but it had to be done. He rang the bell and quickly sprayed some breath freshener. It wouldn't do to stink of booze. When there was no sign of life, he rang the bell again, a long, piercing sound. This time, he saw lights go on and a shadowy figure appeared behind the glass of the front door.

'Who is it?' a woman's voice querulously demanded. 'Is that you, Keith? Have you forgotten your keys again?'

'We're police officers, Mrs Sutherland,' Rafferty shouted back. 'Can you open up, please, we'd like to speak to you.'

The door opened a few inches. Rafferty held up his warrant card in the gap.

Mary Sutherland looked to be in her late fifties. She had short, greying hair that was standing on end. She ran short stubby fingers through it and only managed to increase its disorder. Her ample frame was enveloped in a quilted housecoat in buttercup yellow. She blinked owlishly at them from myopic brown eyes and wiped the sleep from the corners. 'What do you want? What's happened?'

'If we could just come in, Mrs Sutherland, we can explain.'

She opened the door wide and they entered a square, spacious hall. It was a detached house of two stories and with five doors opening off the hall looked to have plenty of room. Rafferty could imagine there must be a huge garden at the rear.

She led the way along the hall and into a nicely proportioned living room with two sets of French windows leading on to a terrace at the rear. There was a group of three large gold-coloured settees grouped around an ornate white marble fireplace. The room was tastefully if conservatively furnished with what looked like original oil paintings of pastoral scenes on the walls.

Mary Sutherland invited them to sit down. Once they were seated, she gazed questioningly at them, her face still dazed from sleep, but with a wary expression in her eyes as if she knew something unwelcome was coming and didn't want to hear it.

Rafferty broke the news. 'It's about your husband. I'm afraid it's bad news.'

'Keith?' The hands resting in her lap gripped each other tightly. 'What do you mean? What's happened to him?'

'I'm afraid he was found earlier this evening in the car park of The Railway Arms public house. He's dead, Mrs Sutherland.' Rafferty was about to add that her husband had been murdered, when she broke in.

'Dead?' she repeated. 'What do you mean? Was it a heart attack?'

The heart had certainly been attacked, Rafferty reflected, though by the blade of a knife rather than from the ravages of an abused middle-aged body. 'No. It wasn't a heart attack. Someone assaulted him.' Unwilling to reveal anything further about the cause of death, he left it at that.

Her mouth opened as if to say something, but no words came out. They sat staring at one another as several seconds ticked away, checked off by the handsome grandfather clock that stood to the right of the door, but it seemed Mrs Sutherland for the moment had nothing to say.

Rafferty broke the silence. 'Is there anyone who could stay with you? A family member, perhaps? Or a friend or neighbour?'

Mary Sutherland continued to stare at him as if she didn't understand what he was saying. But then she seemed to come to herself. 'There's – there's my daughter, Susie. Susan.' She glanced over at the clock. 'But it's very late. I don't like to disturb her at this hour.'

'I'm sure she'd want to be with you at such a time. You shouldn't be alone. I'll get one of my female officers round to her home and fetch her if you'll let me have the address.'

'Yes. Yes, of course.' She rattled off an address and Rafferty gave the nod to Lizzie Green, who went out.

Rafferty heard the door shut behind her. 'I'll make some tea,' he said. He went in search of the kitchen and had the kettle boiled, the teapot found and a tray made up five minutes before Lizzie returned with Mrs Sutherland's daughter.

★ ★ ★

30

Susan Sutherland looked to be in her mid-twenties. She had clearly dressed in a hurry, for the collar of her shirt was half tucked in, her fair hair tousled from the pillow. She went straight to her mother and gave her a tight hug. The older woman clung to her as if she feared what might happen should she let go.

Rafferty gestured to Lizzie and the two of them retreated to the kitchen to leave the grieving women to their privacy.

'There's a son as well,' Rafferty murmured. 'He's on his stag night according to the landlord of The Railway Arms. He's a possible suspect as he had a row with his father just minutes before the elder Sutherland was murdered. God knows where he is. One of the local late-night clubs, presumably. I suppose I could send officers around to the nearest and get them to put out a message on the sound system, but it seems a shame to spoil his night. Bad news can always wait.' That was if it *was* bad news for the son. If he and his father didn't get on, as the information from Andy Strong and the row in the pub had indicated, and he had financial expectations, the news might not be so unwelcome. Always supposing he wasn't guilty of his father's murder himself, which seemed a strong possibility, him being on the spot and all. 'Fine news for him to get, though, in the morning in the midst of a hangover.' He gave a nod towards the living room. 'Perhaps you should get his address from the daughter. But leave it a little while. There's no rush. I don't suppose he'll be home much before dawn.'

Lizzie Green nodded.

'I want you to stay here,' he instructed. 'Be what comfort you can. I'll get back to the pub and see how the team's getting on.'

Rafferty slipped silently out of the front door, closing it gently behind him.

THREE

The following morning brought Dafyd Llewellyn's return to duty, much to Rafferty's relief. He arrived at the police station bright and early, as was his habit. For once, Rafferty, with a busy day ahead of him, had beaten him in. He'd got used to working with the logical Welshman and hadn't relished the first full day of an investigation without his support.

The office they shared, after a week of Rafferty's sole occupation, was untidier than ever, with piles of files and reports teetering precariously on his desk. Llewellyn always kept the office as neat as a new pin and Rafferty noted his sergeant's disapproving expression as Llewellyn returned to the room and took in Rafferty's belated attempts at tidying up. Llewellyn lost his disapproving expression as Rafferty told him about the events of the previous night and the details of those who had already been questioned. Llewellyn read quickly through the witness statements and then shuffled them into a neat pile.

'Right,' said Rafferty, as he sat back in his chair. 'Now you know as much as I do.'

'A vicious mugging, do you think?' Llewellyn asked as he sat at his desk, his intelligent brown gaze fixed on Rafferty. 'I note the victim's wallet was missing.'

'Don't know yet. Could be, of course, though somehow I feel this case is going to turn out to be other than that. There's a smack of something more personal to me. According to the pub landlord, Keith Sutherland was a man good at getting on the wrong side of others. He even had a row with his own son on the boy's stag night, which was held last night at the same pub behind which the body was found. Maybe a coincidence too far, especially as it seems the two didn't get on. Anyway, hopefully we'll have a chance to find out later today.

Meanwhile, we've a pub-full of people to interview more thoroughly. I'm particularly interested in talking to the members of the stag party. I gather they left the pub at the same time as the deceased.'

'Do we know their identities?'

'Only the couple that the landlord was able to give me: the ones who are regulars at The Railway Arms. He didn't know three of the party. But doubtless, we'll have the names and addresses of those three before the day is out.'

'So what do you want to do first?'

'I want to speak to the man who found the body,' Rafferty said. He consulted his notebook. 'He's a Mr David Cookham. Lives here in Elmhurst, on the southern outskirts. He's in the phone book, I checked.' He handed his notebook to Llewellyn. 'His telephone number's in there. Give him a ring and tell him we want to speak to him. Try to arrange it for this morning if possible.'

David Cookham was at home, being a night shift worker at a factory on one of Elmhurst's two industrial estates. He lived in a small flat which, to judge by the number of internal doors off the hall, was a one-bedroomed, one living-roomed apartment. The living room was uncared for; clearly Cookham only regarded the flat as a place to sleep. The furniture was mismatched and looked worn in patches as if it was other people's cast offs. But, Rafferty supposed, if he worked in a factory there wouldn't be much spare cash for new suites of furniture.

By now, Mr Cookham had heard that the man he had found had in fact been dead rather than dead drunk. The realization had clearly shaken him up.

'Last night was my night off. Pretty unlucky to come across a body on my one night off in the week. Guess I could have been the second victim of these guys, these muggers, if I'd left the pub a little earlier.' He rubbed his hand over his face and stared at them from dazed grey eyes from where he sat in a shabby armchair.

'I appreciate that this has been a shock for you, Mr Cookham,' Rafferty said. 'But I'd be grateful if you could try to answer a few questions.'

David Cookham didn't seem to hear him at first, then he shook himself, like an animal trying to remove tormenting fleas. 'Yes, yes, of course. Ask what you want. God, what a thing to have happened. I've ... I've never seen a dead body before. Didn't even realize he was dead. He was laying there in the pub yard, looking as comfortable as if he was stretched out in his own bed.'

35

Rafferty nodded. David Cookham could be no more than his late twenties. It was understandable that the realization that he had seen a dead man should unnerve him.

Cookham clutched his arms round his body, rocking slightly backwards and forwards and gazed at Rafferty as if he expected him to make everything better.

Rafferty broke the silence. 'I know that you found the body, Mr Cookham, but did you see anyone else in the yard? Hear any sound from the street? Car doors slamming or feet running away?'

Cookham shook his head. 'No. I heard nothing. Saw nothing. Strange really, as I saw him leave the pub and he can only have been dead a matter of minutes, if that. Yet the night was quiet. Not a sound anywhere. No one on the street.' Suddenly, he gazed at Rafferty. 'I thought it was funny, some old drunk curled up in Andy's yard. I almost left him there but for the possibility someone would run over him. He looked so peaceful it seemed a shame to have to get Andy to disturb him.' His lips thinned. 'You must think me a fool for not realizing he was dead.'

'No, not at all. It wasn't immediately apparent. Though—' He broke off. He had almost been about to reveal the cause of death and that the wound had bled but

36

little. But these were pieces of evidence he wanted to keep up his sleeve. So far, only Andy Strong and the team knew the cause of death and he wanted it to stay that way. Andy Strong had been warned to keep silent. He wasn't normally a loose-tongued individual, so Rafferty was confident he would keep his counsel. It could be important if they got a suspect who admitted to knifing Sutherland in the back. Such an admission would provide confirmation of guilt, which was always welcome.

'You didn't perhaps hear a car start up as you went back to the pub?'

Cookham shook his head. 'I told you,' he said, 'I heard nothing. Not from the time I left the pub to the time I returned to it to tell Andy about the body. Not a sound. Not a soul. I could pretty much swear there was no one but myself and the drun— the dead man in the yard.'

It was clear that Cookham could tell them nothing more, so they made their goodbyes and left, having arranged for Cookham to come into the station and make an official statement.

'Someone took a hell of a chance,' Rafferty commented as they left Cookham's flat and walked back down the stairs. 'The Railway Arms was almost at chucking out time – they don't go in for this new twenty-four-hour opening like some of the pubs in town, so anyone could have come into the yard at any time. His killer must have been waiting for him, quite cold-bloodedly.'

'Unless it was an opportune mugging, as Mr Cookham thought,' Llewellyn put in. 'Some local tearaway waiting for whomever staggered first round to the car park.'

'I don't know. Something about this killing seems more selective, more deliberate. The knife between the shoulder blades, aimed straight at the heart. There was surely no need for that unless our man wanted his victim dead.'

They reached the car and got in. 'David Cookham must have missed the murderer by seconds. What bad luck he didn't leave the pub a bit earlier and we might have had a description.'

'Or another corpse,' was Llewellyn's cryptic response.

'Mmm. I suppose you're right. I suppose also we ought to be grateful we've only the one of those. Right,' he said. 'Before we see anyone else, let's get over to Ian Sutherland's. I'd like to hear more about the reasons for the argument he had with his late old man. He's likely to be suffering this morning. If he's putting his energies into bearing his hangover, he'll be less likely to have any left to obstruct us, if such is his intention.'

'You think he might want to obstruct us?'

'Yes. He's certainly likely to want to avoid mentioning that he and his father were at loggerheads over his planned marriage. Maybe, also, they had other areas of disagreement. It'll be interesting, shall we say, if he tries to conceal any other disagreements. Let's get over there and drag him from his bed of pain.'

'Have you considered that you might have got this Ian Sutherland all wrong?' Llewellyn murmured as he drove off. 'He's just lost his father – lost him violently and suddenly. Maybe their disagreement is only a temporary thing. Lots of parents don't approve of their children's choice of marital partner.'

'True. Perhaps we're about to find out. Put your foot down.'

Llewellyn putting his foot down wasn't something that happened very often. And it didn't happen now. But they reached their destination eventually. Ian Sutherland lived in a flat on Southgate, about three hundred yards from The Railway Arms. It was no more than a few minutes' drive. Number Sixty-Four was the first-floor flat in a row of terraces. The curtains were still drawn although by now it was ten o'clock.

Rafferty gave three sharp rings on the bell. 'That should wake him up,' he commented.

Llewellyn's lips twitched. 'I'd have thought that you, of all people, would sympathize with a man with a thick head.'

'Oh, I do. But solving this murder has to be my first priority.' He gave another three short bursts to the bell. 'Come on. Come on,' he said. 'Let's be having you.'

Rafferty peered through the letter box and stood back as he saw that his persistent ringing had finally stirred the slothful Ian Sutherland.

The door opened and a bedraggled looking boxer-clad twenty-something male stood on the doorstep and stared at them through eyes that were protectively half-closed against the bright morning light. Rafferty noticed that Ian Sutherland had a bruise on his chin and recalled that someone's fist had connected with flesh last night in the pub. Clearly, it had been the younger Sutherland who had suffered the blow.

Sutherland's plentiful fair hair stood on end. He ran his hand over it in an echo of his mother's similar action the previous night, and, like her, all he succeeded in doing was making it even more disordered. He unglued his eyelids a fraction. 'What do you want? You woke me up.'

'Sorry about that, sir.' Rafferty took out his warrant card and held it up. 'We're police officers, Mr Sutherland. I'm afraid

40

we have some bad news for you. It's concerning your father. May we come in?'

'My father? That old bastard. What's he done?'

Rafferty was surprised that Sutherland's mother or sister hadn't contacted him on his mobile by now to let him know what had happened. Certainly, Sutherland gave a good appearance of ignorance. But then maybe he was a good actor.

'Your father's done nothing, sir. It's what's been done to him.'

'Done to him?'

'If we could just come in, I can explain.'

'Yeah. OK. Come up. You'll excuse me, I hope,' he threw over his shoulder. 'But, as I said, you woke me up. I was on my stag night last night.'

'So I believe.'

Sutherland shot him a strange look as if he didn't understand how Rafferty knew this, but would like to. 'Anyway, it went on pretty late,' he continued as he walked upstairs. 'You could say that too good a time was had by all.' He looked hopefully at each of them in turn as they reached the first floor landing. 'I don't suppose you've got any aspirin?'

'Sorry,' Rafferty replied after Llewellyn, who didn't drink so didn't suffer from hangovers, shook his head. 'My packet's back at the office.'

41

Ian Sutherland gave a groan, clutched his head in his hands, walked along the landing into the living room and slouched on the settee. 'Thank God I booked a day's holiday today. I feel like death.'

It was a surprisingly spacious room and Rafferty guessed the upstairs flat extended over the side alleyway. Furnished in a modern style with pale wooden floors and black leather settees, with cabinets housing a vast selection of CDs and DVDs and a huge plasma television, which dominated the room, hanging from the wall at right angles to the window. It looked what it was: a typical bachelor pad.

Sutherland hadn't bothered either to put on the light or open the blinds so the room was gloomy with only the light from the landing to lessen the dimness.

Rafferty, unwilling to conduct an interview in such Stygian gloom, took it upon himself to raise the blinds. Sutherland let out another groan as he did so and held his hand up in front of his face to shield it from the light. 'Did you have to do that?' he complained. 'You might have a thought for my head. It's splitting.'

'Sorry, sir, but we can't talk in semi-darkness.'

Sutherland sounded sulky as he replied, 'I don't see why not.'

The light from the window revealed the dust gathered on all the flat surfaces of the room, making it look uncared for, as if it was just a place to doss between Ian Sutherland's work and social life. CDs and DVDs were scattered out of their cases on top of the cupboard and also bore a patina of dust.

'Is it all right if we sit down?'

Sutherland gave a grunt, which Rafferty took for acquiescence, and he and Llewellyn sat together on the opposite settee. Llewellyn took out his notebook.

'So what's this all about?'

'As I said, sir, it concerns your father. He was violently attacked last night in the car park of The Railway Arms.'

A wary look crept over Sutherland's face. 'Attacked? Who by?'

'That's what we hope to find out, sir. There's more. I'm afraid your father died as a result of the attack.'

'The old man's dead?' The previously half-closed eyes opened wide. The movement was immediately followed by a groan at such an unwise action. 'How?'

'I'm not at liberty to reveal that at present, sir.' Rafferty paused, then added, 'I understand that you and your friends were celebrating in The Railway Arms yourselves last night?'

Sutherland did not reply for several

seconds. He lay sprawled on the settee with his eyes closed. But then he nodded and opened his eyes as if he realized that it was useless to deny his presence there.

'I understand you saw your father in the public bar?'

'That's right. He'd been in the snug and came into the public bar shortly before eleven. We had a few words, as I imagine you've already found out. The old man tried to gatecrash my stag do. A bit rich, I thought. You'll have heard, or if not, you soon will, that he didn't approve of my forthcoming marriage. Or my choice of bride.'

'Why was that?'

Sutherland gave a bitter laugh, then he winced as if he regretted the incautious laughter. 'He thought Georgie was a gold digger, after his money. Silly old fool. What a laugh that is. See anyone part my father from his cash. Not, according to my mother, that he had any, not any more, not unless he accepted the takeover deal he was offered and there was no chance of that.'

'He was likely to come into a substantial sum of money then, your father, if he'd agreed to the takeover?'

'So he said. Tried telling me he had plenty of the old spondulicks himself, too. Though I suspect he was trying to use the carrot of his supposed cash to keep me and my sister dancing to his tune. It didn't work with either of us. We've both struck out on our own.'

Rafferty, eager to find a possible motive for the son to kill the father, said, 'Maybe he's left you a nice inheritance?'

Sutherland tried another laugh. 'Cut me out of the will, more like.' Suddenly, he stilled and stared at Rafferty. 'Just a minute. I get it. You think I killed him, don't you?'

'Why should we think that, sir?' Rafferty asked blandly. 'Had you cause?'

'No,' he answered sharply, adding, 'nothing but the usual: the old stag and the young one. Locking horns. You know the sort of thing.'

'Did you and your friends leave the pub together?'

'Yes. We went on to a new club in town. Scorpio's. We were there till the early hours. I had no chance to kill the old man. Ask my friends. They'll tell you the same.'

'If I could have the names and addresses of your friends?'

'Going to check my story out? As I said, they'll tell you the same as me. Last we saw of the old man, he was disappearing round to the pub car park. I shouted at him to get a taxi as I could see he'd had a few, but he ignored me.' The realization of his father's death seemed to hit him suddenly, for he sat forward with his hands gripped between his bare thighs and said, 'God. Strange to think he's gone. He seemed indestructible somehow, you know?'

'That's often what children feel when a parent dies, sir. They've always been there, which is, I suppose, why one tends to think that they always will be. If I could have those names and addresses?'

'What? Oh, yes. Right.' He stumbled to his feet, stared bemusedly around him for several seconds then headed towards the phone in the corner where several address and phone books were stacked on top of a cupboard. He shoved the pile of DVDs out of the way and pulled an address book from under them. Slowly, clearly still struggling against a blinding headache, he found the relevant pages and dictated his friends' details, which Llewellyn took down in his notebook.

'Did you see anyone else hanging about before your father walked round to the car park?' Rafferty now asked. 'Any louts, for instance, bent on mugging?'

For a moment, Rafferty thought he was going to clutch at this, but then Sutherland shook his head carefully and said, 'No. I saw no one.'

'Thank you, sir.' Rafferty stood up. 'We'll

let you get on.'

'Get on, nothing. I'm going back to bed.'

'Not going round to see your mother and sister?'

'I'd not be much use to them like this. Better to let them get the weeping and wailing out of the way first. I'll get my head down for a few hours and go over there later. Is that it?'

'Yes, sir. For now. We may need to speak to you again.'

Sutherland nodded. He left them to see themselves out.

As they walked to the car, Rafferty said, 'He didn't seem exactly overcome with grief at the loss of his father, did he?'

'No. He made no attempt to hide it, either.'

'Mmm. I noticed. The nothing-to-hide gambit. Always suspect, to my mind.'

A thin smile hovered over Llewellyn's narrow, aesthetic face. 'Most things are to you.'

'Maybe. But I like to keep my mind open to the possibility of guilt in everyone until the facts prove otherwise. Let's go and see the rest of the stag party boys. Who's nearest?'

Ian Sutherland had given them the workplace as well as the home addresses of the four men who had shared his bachelor party

47

celebration. Rafferty presumed they would all be at work, unless one or more of them had thrown sickies, or, like Sutherland, had had the prescience to book a day's holiday.

Llewellyn consulted the list he had noted down. 'Gavin Harold works here in Elmhurst. The other three work in London.'

Rafferty nodded at the news. He had barely listened to Sutherland's recital of his friends' addresses. 'OK. We'll have to leave them till this evening. Let's get going.'

Gavin Harold worked at a computer software firm on one of the town's two industrial estates: the one situated to the north of the town. It was well before lunchtime and the roads had little in the way of traffic so they made good time.

The weather was still pleasant for early June, which was often a disappointing month. The sun was out, bathing the Essex town's varied buildings in brilliant light, shimmering on the roman bricks that had been pillaged from the town's earlier structures. Elmhurst was an ancient market town with a charter from wicked King John. It had an attractive mix of medieval, Tudor and Georgian buildings, the buildings from each succeeding period fanning out from the mostly medieval centre.

Rafferty sat back and enjoyed the ride: with Llewellyn doing the driving there was plenty of time to do that. He wanted to ask Llewellyn if he had seen Abra since his return from Wales. The two were cousins and pretty close. But the words struggled to form. Part of it was pride. He didn't want to appear needy in front of the Welshman. But, as he had known it would, the hunger to know bit away at the pride, till it was a raggedy-edged nothing. The question when it came was rough and to the point. 'Have you seen Abra?'

Rafferty sensed Llewellyn dart a look towards him. It was made up of a mix of sympathy and exasperation. As if he didn't know he had brought the separation on himself.

'Yes. Maureen and I saw her last night. We stopped by for a little while on our journey home from Wales.'

Llewellyn and Mo, his wife, had been visiting Llewellyn's mother, Gloria, at her home in Gwynedd for the past week.

Rafferty had met Gloria and had liked her. A former dancer, her pairing with Llewellyn's late father, a Methodist minister, had always struck him as incongruous.

'How was she?'

'Abra was her usual self at first, but then she turned tearful. She asked after you.'

'Did she?' Rafferty could barely contain his delight at this revelation. 'What did she say?'

'Not much. Just wanted to know if you were well. And if you missed her.'

'And what did *you* say?'

'That you did miss her. And were sorry for what you'd done.'

'And how did she take that?'

'Better than she had on the previous occasions on which I've spoken to her. She now accepts that she went a bit over the top on the wedding arrangements and that you were merely trying to limit the financial burden she was taking on for you both.'

'Does she? Really? That's a result.'

'Yes. And she means it, too, Joseph. She seemed a little shamefaced at her previous extravagance.'

'So the wedding's back on?' Rafferty demanded eagerly.

Llewellyn's lips pursed. 'Let's not rush too far ahead.' He slowed down for the traffic lights, even though they had only just turned to amber.

Rafferty, champing at every bit, choked down an involuntary protest.

'She's agreed to meet you,' Llewellyn told him once he had engaged the handbrake and put the gear lever into neutral.

'When? Where?'

'At The Red Lion in the High Street, on Sunday week. With Maureen and myself as mediators.'

This last was said with a voice on the downturn as if it wasn't a role Llewellyn relished.

Rafferty felt a guilty pang that Llewellyn had been dragged into the fallout of his and Abra's relationship bust-up. But the Welshman had offered to mediate; it wasn't as if he had twisted his arm. Still, a bit of flattery always helped. 'It's good of you to do that, Dafyd,' Rafferty began falteringly. 'I'm grateful.'

'I don't see that we have much choice if we're to break the impasse.' Practical, logical as ever, Llewellyn voiced the nub of the matter.

And it was true. Rafferty knew that, without Llewellyn, he and Abra would never have got this close to reconciliation. Instead, they'd just have drifted further apart on the wings of their pride.

'I suggested a meeting time of one o'clock and Abra agreed. I'd also suggest you stick to mineral water and eschew alcohol.'

Even while his heart soared with the hope that fuelled it, Rafferty felt a quiet amusement at his educated sergeant's choice of language. Who else in the world would use the word 'eschew'? And even though he wasn't entirely sure of the meaning, he got the gist.

At last, the traffic lights turned to green. Llewellyn let out the brake, engaged first gear and changed the subject. 'How do you want to tackle the interview with Gavin Harold?'

'What?' Bemused, Rafferty dragged his mind back from contemplating his burgeoning hopes of a reconciliation with Abra and fixed them on the current murder investigation. 'I suppose I'm mainly interested in discovering if Ian Sutherland hung back when they left the pub on the excuse of going to the gents'. If he had a chance, even just a few minutes, to run round to the car park and murder his father.'

'Surely he'll have primed his friends to say nothing if he did so?'

'Maybe. Maybe not. Maybe he was relying on the amnesiac qualities of alcohol to clear it from their minds. But if they do recall such a hanging back, they might tell us about it. I'm relying on one of them to let the cat out of the bag, if, indeed, there's a pussy concealed in it.'

'Especially if one of them also had good reason to wish Keith Sutherland dead.'

'Yes.' They were crossing Tiffey Reach over the River Tiffey and almost at their destination. Rafferty stared out of the window at the sluggish waters below, thinking about the interview ahead and how best to tackle it. But it didn't prevent his eye for a pretty girl from noticing that the sunshine had brought the early lunchtime crowd out. A few young girls in their scanty summer clothes were walking along the towpath. He wondered what Abra was wearing and who was eyeing her up. The thought made him downcast. He was glad when they reached the forecourt of Software Solutions, the firm where Gavin Harold worked, and parked up.

The computer firm was housed in a low-rise office block of two stories, next to a vehicle repair workshop. Rafferty was surprised the building was as large as it was, having assumed that software companies required only a few whizz-kids and a bank of computer hardware to run their businesses.

They got out of the car and walked over to the double-glass doors at the entrance.

The receptionist behind the desk was as up-to-the-minute as the line of business. Spiky hair that was all the colours of the rainbow, perched above a face that was engaged in an animated phone conversation as they entered the lobby.

She glanced at them, said, 'I'll call you back,' and replaced the phone on its rest. She asked how she could help once they'd reached the desk and if they had an appointment when Rafferty told her they wanted to see Gavin Harold.

'We're police officers, miss.' He flashed his warrant card. 'I doubt we'll keep him long.'

'One moment. I'll see if he's available.'

He'd better be, thought Rafferty, averse to the possibility of a computer geek thinking he could avoid the inevitable interview by being 'engaged'.

He'd been engaged, with a not-too-far-in-the-future wedding in the offing. And now he'd have to wait the long days till the following Sunday to find out if his engagement to Abra was on again. Not to mention the wedding.

Apparently Gavin Harold had thought twice about giving them the runaround, for he was waiting on the first floor as they rounded the stairs and extended his hand in a welcoming gesture. He was dressed casually in cream chinos and a black T-shirt with the company's logo picked out in white. He had untidy ginger hair that ran to wild curls and currently had a pen perched among the tresses. Rafferty thought you could probably lose a dozen in such a bird's nest. Gavin Harold shifted from foot to foot as Rafferty made the introductions, as if he couldn't wait to get back to his computer. This impression increased as he hurried, in a bandy-legged walk, down the corridor and

54

made a swift left turn through an open office door. It was a big room, full of computer monitors, as Rafferty had imagined.

Gavin Harold gave a yearning glance at the hardware, but then, seeming to shrink into himself, he led them across to a conversation area squashed into the corner that consisted of one large suede sofa and an armchair in the same material. There was a water cooler on a glass coffee table to the side of the seating, but no cups.

'How can I help you?' he asked as he threw himself into the armchair.

Rafferty didn't bother with any preamble. 'I don't know whether you've heard, but Ian Sutherland's father was killed last night. Murdered.'

Gavin Harold nodded. 'Ian rang a few minutes ago and told me about it.'

So they'd had the chance to put together matching stories of the events of the previous night.

'We wondered what you could tell us. You'll know, of course, that Mr Sutherland died in the car park of The Railway Arms?'

Harold nodded.

'You were there, were you not? You and your friends. At Ian Sutherland's stag party?'

Harold nodded again, but added nothing more. Rafferty wondered if he was going to

55

have to drag his story from him. 'Tell me about it.'

Harold shrugged. 'Not much to tell, really. We'd arranged to meet at the pub at eight thirty and—'

'By "we" you mean yourself, Ian Sutherland, Chris Tennant, Rick Wentworth and Sanjay Gupta?'

'Yes. As you know, it was Ian's stag do. From there, we went on into the centre of town to the Scorpio Club.'

'If we can just backtrack a bit.' To forestall the possibility of Gavin Harold believing he could get away with any lies, he said, 'We're informed that Ian Sutherland's father came into the public bar from the snug close to eleven o'clock and there was an argument between him and Ian.'

'Hardly an argument. There wasn't time before the landlord chucked the lot of us out. He was a bit the worse for wear. As, no doubt, were we.' He gave a short laugh.

'I see. And what happened then?'

Harold gave another shrug. 'Nothing much, apart from a bit of ineffectual fisticuffs from Daddy Sutherland before we were all chucked out. Ian's dad walked round to the car park and we headed into town.'

'All of you?'

'Yes. All of us. We headed into town together and were together for the rest of the night. The others will tell you the same. Ian didn't kill his dad, if that's what you're thinking. He didn't have the opportunity. Neither did any of the rest of us.'

'And none of you hung back? To go to the gents', say?'

'No, Inspector. We'd all already gone to the gents. We were keen to get to Scorpio's and have a few tequila slammers. Get the evening going properly.'

'You seem none the worse for it this morning, Mr Harold,' Rafferty observed. 'Unlike your friend, Mr Sutherland, who went back to bed after we spoke to him.'

Harold grinned. It gave his whole face an impish quality. 'That's because I spewed my ring when we left the club. Got rid of the lot in a drain. Unlike Ian. But he was the stag lad. It's tradition that he have a bad head the morning after.'

Whether Harold was telling them the truth about the five friends leaving the pub together, Rafferty didn't know, but it was clear the young man wasn't going to tell them anything different, so they made their goodbyes and left.

'Well, we didn't get much change out of him,' Rafferty grumbled as they got back in the car. 'Suppose we can expect the same story from Sutherland's other three friends.'

'Seems likely. Maybe he was telling the truth?'

'Maybe he was. We need a bit of background, Dafyd. We need to find out if there was more to the father and son falling out than Ian Sutherland's choice of bride. Maybe we'll get it out of his sister.'

'I don't think we should just be concentrating on the family, although I agree we need to check for any other reasons for family argument.'

'I'm not going to be just concentrating on the family,' Rafferty protested. 'According to Andy Strong, the landlord of The Railway Arms, old man Sutherland had a talent for falling out with people. So another thing we ought to look into is just who else he had these fallings out with. Remind me to collect the list from Andy Strong. He should have finished it by now.' He did up his seat belt before Llewellyn mentioned it.

'Let's get along to Keith Sutherland's home and see what we can learn there. I want to find out about his work and his friends and enemies both.'

Llewellyn nodded, did up his own seat belt and started the car. He reversed neatly and soon they were heading back up the bypass to the Sutherlands' home.

FOUR

Lizzie Green had already been relieved of her role as Family Liaison Officer and had left the Sutherlands' home by the time Rafferty and Llewellyn reached it. In her place was Claire Allen, a young PC and the newest member of the team. Rafferty had a quick chat with her, but after she had updated him on her own and Lizzie Green's time in the house he had learned nothing significant. She ushered them into the living room and closed the door behind them.

There was no sign of Mrs Sutherland, but her daughter was still there, looking wrung out and heavy-eyed as if she had slept badly.

'My mother's asleep,' she told them as soon as they entered the room. 'The doctor gave her some sleeping pills and I insisted she take them.'

'That's all right, Miss Sutherland. We wouldn't dream of disturbing her. Perhaps you can answer a few questions?'

Susan Sutherland was fair like her brother. She wore her hair to the shoulders in the rats' tails look that seemed to be current amongst young women. Rafferty wondered how much she'd paid for the styling. The ends were dyed a darker colour than the rest. The style gave her the look of a racoon. Or did he mean a skunk? Some two-toned animal, anyway. She still wore the same clothes that she had thrown on the previous night, though he presumed she'd combed her hair since he'd last seen her. She seemed restless. Once she'd invited them to sit, she got up and wandered to the window and back again.

She ignored his request that she answer some questions and instead, as she came to a halt in front of Rafferty, asked if there was any news.

'It's early days yet, Miss Sutherland. We'll be sure to tell you as soon as we learn anything.'

'Susie, please.'

'Little enough news yet, Susie, as I said. Only that your brother's got a king-sized hangover.'

'Nothing new there, then.' She paused. 'As you said, I suppose it's too soon for any developments. My father only died last night. You will tell us when you have some news? Any news.'

'Of course. How's your mother been?'

She had perched on the arm of the settee

60

she had been sitting on, but now she jumped up again. 'About how you'd expect her to
be. She *has* just lost her husband.'

Rafferty nodded and returned to his
previous request. 'Perhaps you could tell me
something of your father? We need to know
as much as we can about him, his work, his
friends, his enemies, if we're to catch his
murderer. I understand he didn't approve of
your brother's fiancée.'

'My father didn't approve of a lot. He'd
have come round. Eventually.'

'I understand your father had his own
business?'

'Yes. He has – had – a partner. Derek
Fowler. They were in business together for
twenty years.'

They obtained Fowler's address and that
of the business before Rafferty gestured for
her to go on.

'As for friends, my father didn't have a
great talent for friendship. He had a greater
talent for losing friends than making them.'

'If you could let us have a few names?'

She rattled several off with details of
where they lived and went quiet again.

'And enemies?' Rafferty prompted. 'Did
he have any of those?'

Susie Sutherland slumped down again on
the arm of the chair. 'No. I wouldn't call
them enemies. Not the sort who'd kill him,

61

anyway. As I said, he's got more ex-friends than most people, but that's all. I can't think of anyone who'd go as far as killing him.'

Rafferty had hoped for more. But at least he had a few names to be going on with. Maybe he'd learn more from Sutherland's business partner and from his ex-friends. It was clear that Sutherland Senior hadn't confided details of any potential killing enemies to his daughter – not that he'd really expected her to provide such information.

'What happens now?' she asked. 'My mother and I were wondering about the funeral.'

'We'll let you know when the coroner releases the body. But it'll be some time yet. There'll have to be a post-mortem and an inquest. I'm afraid violent death, such as your father's, inevitably complicates matters.'

'I see. Of course. I hadn't thought.' She paused, then asked reluctantly, 'Do you want me to identify the body?'

'I ... er ... I thought perhaps your brother could do that.'

She gave a short laugh. 'Ian? I doubt if his stomach's up to it. I'm perfectly willing to do it. I can come now, if you like.'

Rafferty nodded. 'If you're sure.' She seemed positively blasé about the prospect of identifying her father, which struck him as decidedly cold-blooded.

'I'll just get my coat. Will the policewoman stay here in case my mother wakes up? I don't want her to be left alone at the moment.'

'Of course.'

Susie Sutherland disappeared into the hall and returned wearing a thin raincoat of grey gaberdine. 'It won't take long, will it?' she asked, suddenly subdued as if just realizing the unpleasantness of the task she had so readily taken on. 'Only I would prefer to be here for my mother as much as possible.'

'No. It won't take long at all. Your father's body's at Elmhurst General. We can have you there and back in half an hour.'

'Good. Shall we go? I'd like to get it over with.'

She led them out the door at a brisk pace and after Rafferty opened the rear door of their car she climbed in without a word, a silence she kept up all the way to the mortuary.

She was equally brisk when it came to identifying her father. After initially going pale and taking a gulp of air, she said, 'Yes,' when the mortuary assistant drew back the sheet covering the body. 'That's him. That's my father. Strange,' she said in a wondering tone, 'but he looks softer somehow. Less—'

She broke off as if conscious she had been about to speak ill of the dead and was unwilling to voice the thought.

Less what? Rafferty wondered. Belligerent? Argumentative? Whatever she had been going to say was left hanging in the air. But one thing seemed clear: she was apparently in no more deep mourning for the dead man than was his son.

It was rather sad. At least Keith Sutherland's wife had had the grace to take to her bed, though they still didn't have any clear idea how she felt about her husband's death.

They drove Susie Sutherland back to her mother's home and left her there to cope as best she could with the assistance of Claire Allen and made for the station. Rafferty was keen to see if anything new had come in during their absence.

But when they arrived at the station and made their way to the incident room, they were quickly updated by Mary Carmody, who told them that nothing valuable had so far come in, though they'd had plenty of the usual crank calls since the news of the murder had gone out on local radio and television.

'The statements from the pub customers and from the house-to-house enquiries are on your desk, sir.'

Oh joy, thought Rafferty, as he contemplated the thought of the heaped piles of probably nothing very much that were waiting for him. 'Best get to it, then,' he said with a forced smile. 'Any news from Dr Dally yet? He said he hoped to do the postmortem this morning.'

Mary nodded. 'He rang. But he'll be doing the PM this afternoon rather than this morning. He wondered if he should hold fire till you get there.'

Same old Sam, thought Rafferty. Looking for the sadist's pound of flesh. It was Rafferty's poorly kept secret that he loathed being present at PMs. The bloody dismemberment of yet another corpse being the last thing he ever fancied witnessing. 'I'll ring him.'

He headed for his office, trailed by Llewellyn. Soon, they were both deeply immersed in the statements, Rafferty only breaking off in order to ring Dally and make his excuses.

'Bottling it, Rafferty?' Sam Dally teased when he was called to the phone.

'Not at all. I'm snowed under with paperwork, is all. I'll look forward to your report. Must get on. Bye Sam.'

He replaced the receiver and gave a relieved sigh, but not before he heard the earthy sound of sardonic laughter echoing down the line. Bloody man, he thought. How's he

65

so unerringly able to pick up on my weak points? Telephone excuses made and laughter over, he settled back to reading the reports. But his diligence was rewarded within another five minutes when he picked up the next statement on the pile.

'Here, Daff,' he said as he handed the statement over. 'Have a look at that. It looks like Ian Sutherland may have some explaining to do.'

The statement, from a Mr Harry Longman, said he had been in the gents' of The Railway Arms close on eleven and was leaving when he bumped into Ian Sutherland in the gap between the inner and outer doors to the gents' toilet. His statement said it seemed as if Ian was undecided whether he was coming or going.

The witness claimed Sutherland had still been there when he had gone back to the bar.

'Wonder if this episode was before or after the landlord slung him and his friends and father out? We'll have to speak to this witness, see if we can't get his timing more precise. But I know it was ten fifty-five p.m. when the landlord threw them all out. I looked at the clock above the bar, so it's going to be a close-run thing.'

'Would he have long enough, though, once this witness had returned to the bar, to run round to the car park, locate and kill his father, and catch up with his friends?'

'How long would it take? No more than a few minutes, as long as there was no hesitation or holding back. In with the knife and off. As quick as that. Yes, we definitely ought to have another word with the hung-over Ian Sutherland. But before we do that, I want to speak to his other three friends and see if one of them drops him in it. But in the meantime, I'd like us to break the back of these statements. I don't want to leave them till we've got another mountain of the blasted things to get through.'

During the next three hours, they buckled down and worked their way through the piles of paper, though they found no more nuggets like that from Harry Longman.

Still, thought Rafferty, they'd had their reward. The only trouble was that by the time they questioned him again, Ian Sutherland was likely to have recovered from his hangover and regained his wits. He'd already let slip that there had been antagonism between himself and his father. But how likely was it now that he'd let slip anything else? Indeed, he'd probably backtrack and declare that they'd misunderstood the bad feeling between himself and his father. But it couldn't be helped. And whatever Sutherland said, Rafferty knew what he'd heard

67

and how it had been expressed, however much Sutherland might, in sobriety, try to gloss over the words used.

They would just have to wait and see what else was out there to be discovered.

FIVE

Rafferty was in his office when the phone rang later that afternoon. It was Dr Sam Dally with the post-mortem results on Keith Sutherland.

'It's much as I told you at the scene. There's little to add except that it was a single-bladed knife, at least eight inches long. The victim died from one knife thrust straight to the heart,' he reported. 'Either our killer was an expert or he got lucky.'

'You say "he", but—'

'Could equally well be a she. Choose your spot and it would have gone through like a blade through butter as it seems to have done in this instance. The estimated time of death remains the same.'

'Any idea what sort of knife?'

'A kitchen knife would be my guess. A carver, well sharpened. The sort you can find in every kitchen.'

Great, thought Rafferty. Just what I need – nothing to narrow it down at all.

After thanking Sam, he hung up and sat staring broodingly at the phone. Maybe the kitchen knife ruled out Ian Sutherland and his friends. Young men tended to favour knives other than kitchen utensils for their assaults.

There again, maybe it was how he was meant to think and his suspicions were being manipulated away from the young men. Either way, time and the continuing investigation would hopefully reveal the truth.

The day was another busy one with Rafferty setting the investigatory team in various directions. He spent most of it ploughing through piles of paperwork, trying to get a handle on anything that looked like a clue. But other than Mr Longman's sighting of Ian Sutherland in the doorway of the gents' toilet at The Railway Arms, there were none of these. They would speak to that young man again and find out what he had to say for himself. But, in the meantime, it was on with the paperwork. He found if he didn't deal with this on a daily basis the molehill soon became a mountain.

★ ★ ★

That evening, Rafferty and Llewellyn did the rounds of Ian Sutherland's other friends: Chris Tennant, Rick Wentworth and Sanjay Gupta.

They started with Tennant. He lived in an apartment in Elmhurst to the west of the town, overlooking the ancient priory ruins in Priory Park. Tennant must have a good job because not only was his home in an enviable position, it was also spacious and expensively furnished, from the ornate granite fireplace in the main room to the large and original artworks on the plain white walls. There was a huge expanse of window, extending the full length of one wall. It must make the room very light and airy earlier in the day. But now, all they could see was a magnificent sunset of swirling orange and crimson off to the left. Although the room's electric lights were dimmed they couldn't conceal Chris Tennant's bloodshot eyes and deathly pallor.

Poor sod, thought Rafferty as he had a moment's fellow feeling for a sufferer from the demon drink.

'So what's this about, Inspector?' Tennant asked as he slumped in one of his deep leather armchairs. 'You said something on the phone about Ian Sutherland.'

'Yes, sir. Mr Sutherland's father was murdered last night. I'm surprised you haven't heard it on the news.'

Tennant pulled a face. 'I decided on a quiet day today, with no radio or TV. I've been nursing the most damnable hangover. Worst one I can remember.' He paused. 'You said Ian's father was murdered. God, that's awful.' His shock seemed genuine. 'I can't believe it.'

Rafferty gave an understanding nod. 'How did it happen?'

'We're not at liberty to reveal that at present.' He quickly outlined the events of the previous evening.

Tennant shook his head as if he still couldn't believe it. 'God. What a shock. Poor Ian.'

'He hasn't contacted you at all today?'

'Obviously not.' He gestured towards a huge black leather sofa. 'Please. Sit down.' When they were seated, he asked, 'So why are you here exactly? I don't understand.'

'I believe you were one of the party at Ian Sutherland's stag night at The Railway Arms?'

'Yes. Ian and I are good friends. We've known each other since school. How's he taking it?'

'He seems less shocked than you, sir.'

Tennant laughed, but immediately seemed to regret his humour. 'That sounds like Ian. Not much of a one for showing his feelings.

Inside, he'll be gutted.'

'I was under the impression that Mr Sutherland didn't get on with his father,' Rafferty commented, hoping to extract some juice from the tale.

'They've had their ups and downs, like most fathers and sons. Ian always got on better with his mother.'

'Tell me about when you left the pub. Did any member of the party lag behind?'

'Lag behind? With the prospect of tequila slammers spurring us on? I should say not. Certainly not as I recall.' His lips pulled back as if he was about to give another laugh, but clearly he thought better of it because the laugh died on his lips. 'Not that I can recall a lot about last night. Must have had a good time. My head certainly tells me I did.'

'You're sure that no one lagged behind as you left?' Rafferty persisted. 'To visit the gents', perhaps?'

'I'm as sure as I can be, which isn't one hundred per cent, unfortunately. I'm afraid you'll need to ask the others. I can only hope they're able to help more than I can.' He frowned suddenly, then said, 'Hold on. I've been very slow, haven't I? Asking if anyone lagged behind. God, you think Ian killed his old man, don't you? Christ, how can you think that? There might have been differences of opinion between them, but their relationship wasn't that bad.'

'At this stage we have to investigate every possibility, however unlikely. We need to eliminate him and you and the rest of your friends, that's all. Once we do that, we can concentrate on those that remain.'

Tennant seemed shocked that he should be included amongst the suspects in a murder enquiry – far more so than had Gavin Harold or Ian Sutherland himself.

Rafferty stood up. 'If you can't help us any further, we'll leave you to enjoy the rest of your evening.'

Tennant also stood up. 'I wish I could help you more. I just don't remember much of the evening. Maybe more will come back if I think about it.'

Rafferty handed him a card. 'Give me a call if it does.'

'Of course. Let me see you out.'

As the apartment door closed behind them, Rafferty muttered, 'Well, that was a waste of time. Let's hope the other two can tell us more.'

Luckily, Rick Wentworth and Sanjay Gupta both lived near one another. Not that either of them proved any more helpful than had Chris Tennant. Both pleaded alcoholic amnesia; a handy crutch to save them having to lie. If, that was, they had any need to lie.

It was nearly nine o'clock by the time they came out of Sanjay Gupta's flat.

'This is going well,' Rafferty commented. 'Let's hope we have better luck tomorrow.'

'We've still to see the people on the list that Andy Strong drew up.' Rafferty had sent one of the uniformed officers to collect the list earlier that day and do preliminary interviews. 'Not to mention Keith Sutherland's former friends. Maybe they can add some illumination on the victim.'

'Mmm. I've had it for tonight, anyway,' said Rafferty. 'They'll have to wait till tomorrow.'

They returned to the station, wrote up their reports and went their separate ways – Llewellyn home to Maureen and Rafferty back to his empty flat. He went via St Mark's Road, which was where Abra had her flat. The place was in darkness and he tortured himself with wondering where she might be. And who she might be with. Abra wasn't an early bird so it was unlikely that she'd gone to bed. She was out on the town somewhere, with someone, enjoying herself, while he was behaving like some sad-git stalker.

Better get home, Rafferty told himself, in case she returns early and finds you watching her flat. That wouldn't go down too well.

He turned the wheel and drove his lonely furrow home. He must just hope that something positive came out of their meeting on Sunday week.

Rafferty had thought the previous day had brought little promising in the way of evidence, though at least his wasn't the only investigation doing a go-slow. But he discovered that this happy state of affairs had undergone a change when he arrived at the station.

Bill Beard was on desk duty in reception and said to him as soon as he set foot across the threshold, 'You won't have heard.'

'Heard what? I've just got in.'

'About those electrical warehouse thefts. We've got a suspect. He's being questioned in interview room one now.'

The news was unwelcome for more reasons than one of professional jealousy. 'What was it? A hot tip from a grass?'

'Yes. One of Tom Kendall's snouts came up trumps. They're looking for the other two suspects he named now.'

Rafferty wasn't on the team that was investigating the electrical warehouse thefts. He'd been otherwise engaged with a murder enquiry when the first of the thefts had occurred in April. He'd have to catch Tom Kendall later and get up to speed. With his mother as a probable buyer of stolen goods, he was in a definite need-to-know situation.

Keith Sutherland had been sixty-eight when he died and though over retirement age had still been working, so Rafferty presumed his ex-friends were of a similar vintage.

After he and Llewellyn had read that morning's reports, they got themselves over to the first of these ex-friends, Gilbert Fortescue.

They found Fortescue in his front garden. He lived in a large, semi-detached with early roses rambling over the front of the house. Rafferty quickly told him why they were there.

Gilbert Fortescue was a small man, no more than five foot six, with a lined brown face that betokened a lot of time spent in the open air. He didn't beat about the bush once Rafferty had finished the explanation for their visit, but said simply,

'I suppose you want me to dish the dirt.'

It was a statement rather than a question and was said in a world-weary manner as though Fortescue had already responded to similar requests.

'I've had the press here for half the morning,' he told them. 'God knows how they got my name or my former connection to Keith. I couldn't get rid of them until I told them what they wanted to hear.'

'Which was?'

'That my late and former friend was a randy devil where the women were concerned. I caught him trying it on with my granddaughter once, which is the reason we fell out. Shouldn't crap on your own doorstep is my philosophy, which is what I told him. He didn't like it. We had something of a shouting match and he stormed off. That was the last I saw of him. Not much of a one for apologizing, Keith.'

'When was this?' Rafferty asked.

'About ten months ago. I came home unexpectedly one afternoon and caught him with my granddaughter backed into a corner and him slobbering all over her. He got a shock when I appeared, I can tell you. Cooled his ardour pretty smartly.'

It was an interesting new light on the victim. It also opened up other possibilities re the investigation. Maybe the father or husband of another of Sutherland's fancies had taken even greater exception to his behaviour than had Fortescue.

'And that's the only reason you fell out?'

'Reason enough, I'd have thought. Particularly as my granddaughter was only seventeen at the time.' Fortescue snipped his secateurs with unnecessary vigour at a withered section of rose bush. 'Keith's fallen out with a few friends over the years. Never one to respect boundaries, was Keith. Thought everyone's wife and daughter were fair game. I'm surprised it's taken till now for someone to attack him.'

Fortescue was able to tell them little more beyond the information that he had been at home with his wife all the previous evening. After checking with Mrs Fortescue they left him to his roses and went to see the next ex-friend on their list, one Randolph Hurley.

Hurley was as different again from Gilbert Fortescue as it was possible for one man to be from another. Around the same, mid-sixty age, he was tall, slim and lived with his wife in a top-floor flat in the centre of town. The flat was sparsely furnished, with the bare minimum of seating and a couple of thin but expensive-looking rugs on the floor. He had also been at home all the previous evening as his wife readily confirmed.

'I heard about Keith Sutherland's murder on the local news,' Hurley volunteered. 'Cannot say I'm surprised. The man went out of his way to court angry reactions.' He gazed at Rafferty over a pair of slim, gold-framed spectacles. 'I imagine you must have learned that much by now.'

'How do you mean that he went out of his way?' Rafferty asked, keeping to himself the knowledge of Sutherland's womanizing.

'I don't want to speak ill of the dead, but let's just say he did his best to spread his attentions amongst the fair sex more than was prudent. Never good at taking no for an answer was Keith.'

'Do you know of anyone he had been actively pursuing recently?' Llewellyn asked.

'No. Not now. Haven't set eyes on him in months. Though there was a time when he'd relish telling one all about his doings. Thought me a dried-up old stick who needed titillating. I never encouraged him. Not that he needed encouragement. It was stopping him that was the problem. No, you need to speak to Carol Mumford. She's been his mistress for years and knew how to keep tabs on Keith and his doings. She'll probably be able to tell you who was Keith's latest fancy and whether the husband had found out about it. I presume that's the sort of information you're after?'

Rafferty nodded. 'And where can we find this Ms Mumford?' he enquired.

Hurley told them and Llewellyn made a note of the address.

'Sutherland sounds to have been a right randy old goat,' Rafferty observed as they got in the lift and returned to the ground floor. 'Sounds like there could have been any number of irate husbands after his blood. Let's hope this Carol Mumford kept as good tabs on her lover as Hurley said. Hopefully, we'll get the names of a few other potential suspects.'

'That's if she's willing to admit she was Sutherland's mistress.'

'Why wouldn't she? It must be common knowledge. Hurley said they'd been an item for years. The old reliable. The one he came back to when he'd a knock-back from other women or their husbands made their objections painfully clear. Must be a heap of resentment there.'

Carol Mumford lived not far from Sutherland, on the sixth floor of a block of flats, which gave her a bird's-eye view of Sutherland's house.

'Nice and handy for a quick drop of how's your father,' was Rafferty's comment. 'Handy, too, for her to keep an eye on him and his comings and goings. Near enough to torture her, too, most likely, if she cared for him. Revenge of the woman spurned, do you think, Daff?'

'As far as we know, he hadn't spurned her, just kept her as his old faithful – there when the world became too hot for him. Still, not an enviable position for her.'

'Bit like a comfort blanket.'

They got in the lift and pressed six. The lift creaked and groaned a bit, but eventually stopped and they got out and walked along to Number Sixty-Two.

Rafferty was surprised by the appearance of the woman who answered the door. He'd more or less expected a bleached blonde, blowsy barmaid type. But Carol Mumford was discreetly dressed in clothes that covered her up to the throat and down to the knees. She wore her light-brown hair in an elegant chignon and looked more like an old-fashioned schoolmarm than the long-term mistress of a man like Keith Sutherland.

Her eyes were red-rimmed, as was her nose and she clutched a tissue tightly as if to guard against more tears. She seemed to be the only one to genuinely mourn Sutherland.

They were soon ensconced in her living room – a room decorated in soothing pastel colours and comfortable cream settees.

She sat down on the settee opposite the two policemen, her back wonderfully straight, and said, 'I wondered when you'd get around to seeing me.'

'We only learned of your existence this morning, Ms Mumford,' Rafferty explained. 'I'm sorry for your loss. I understand that you and Mr Sutherland were friends for a number of years.'

'Fifteen years, four months and ten days,' she replied.

Rafferty judged her to be in her mid-forties, so she must have been around thirty when she became Sutherland's mistress. It was a long time to play second fiddle to his wife and third, fourth and twentieth lady friends and to give up on a husband and children of her own. He had met such self-sacrificing women before and was always astonished at their forbearance, astonished, too, at the men for whom they were willing to forego the normal pleasures of life. Martyrs, he considered them. Fools, too. But Carol Mumford struck him as neither. She seemed a self-sufficient woman, with her own home and presumably her own career. Being a mistress must suit her. At least she didn't have to do her lover's laundry, though it must have made for many a lonely Christmas.

'You must have known Mr Sutherland well,' Rafferty began.

'Come, Inspector, let's not be coy.' She met his eyes directly and he was the one to feel uncomfortable. 'I was his long-term mistress, not his best buddy. I'm going to miss him.'

'How often did you see him?'

'Usually a couple of times a week, sometimes less. It was a flexible arrangement.'

'A lonely one, too, I should think.'

She lowered her head in acquiescence, but

didn't break out into a bout of self-pity. She had chosen her path in life, her expression seemed to say, and she would live with it.

'Did Mr Sutherland speak to you of any enemies he had? Or of anyone who had threatened him?'

She gave a faint smile as if she found his question slightly naive. 'No. Not the sort you mean, anyway. He'd hardly discuss the husbands he'd cuckolded with me. And yes, I knew about the other women. Not that there were as many as Keith would have liked. He had a tendency to overestimate his own charms, particularly with younger women. Not that there have been so many of those lately. Age had taken its toll on Keith's libido. He just went through the motions. I think he was more relieved than anything when his come-ons weren't taken up. No, I don't think it was an irate husband who killed him. Not now. What he did talk about was his business life, rivals, his partner, that sort of thing.'

'Oh yes. His business partner. What can you tell me about him?'

'Derek Fowler and Keith were in the same line – electrical wholesale – and they decided to team up. It worked well for twenty years, but the business has done badly lately. Too much competition from the Far East.'

'You said it worked well for twenty years. I

sensed a "but".'

'Perspicacious of you. Yes, lately there's been a "but". The firm had a much larger concern interested in taking them over, buying them out. It would have meant a hefty sum of money for both of them. Plenty to retire on, which I understand is the reason Derek wanted to accept the offer. But Keith had no interest in retiring. He and Derek Fowler had a major falling-out a few weeks before Keith's death.' Again, she met Rafferty's gaze squarely even if she had faltered slightly in mentioning Sutherland's demise. She told him simply, 'I think it possible you wouldn't need to look much further than Derek Fowler for your murderer. In his way, he could be as ruthless as Keith.'

It was an interesting theory and one Rafferty knew he must investigate as soon as possible. But he found it interesting also that Carol Mumford should be so ready to point the finger. Had she simply wanted to help them find the killer? Or had she some other end in view?

After all, she was now approaching fifty and had played the role of Sutherland's mistress *en titre*, his comfort blanket, for fifteen years. Maybe she'd grown tired of the role and the younger extras dogging her heels. Maybe she'd put an ultimatum to

Sutherland and been rebuffed. She would not be the first mistress to want revenge. Wouldn't be the first to decide that if she couldn't have her lover, no one else would.

All of which thoughts he confided to Llewellyn when they were back in the car, having ascertained that Carol Mumford had been at home alone the previous evening.

'But why would she choose to kill him now?' Llewellyn objected. 'Nothing would appear to have changed. We've no evidence that Sutherland had tossed her aside.'

'She's approaching the menopause for one thing. Women can get funny ideas in their heads when they're a certain age. Maybe she was regretting all the things she's missed out on – marriage, kids, a happy home life – and blamed her lover.'

'Possibly. But she's accepted her situation for years and must also have accepted that Sutherland wasn't prepared to offer her more. Though, I agree, she was over eager to give us Derek Fowler as a suspect.'

'Makes you wonder if she has reason to hold a grudge against Fowler.'

'Perhaps we should visit Mr Fowler next and see if we can find out what it might be.'

'Good idea, Daff. I do like a straightforward motive and given this nice little earner takeover that was in the offing, it would seem our Mr Fowler, at least, offers us that. Let's get over there and see what he has to say for himself.'

Llewellyn turned on the ignition, engaged first gear and released the brake. Then he sat there for an inordinate length of time waiting for a gap in the traffic.

Rafferty gritted his teeth impatiently, frustrated that while he was anxious to interview Fowler, Llewellyn could waste time dilly-dallying and waiting for a hundred-yard space before he emerged from the spot.

SIX

But Derek Fowler wasn't in his office. They learned from his secretary that he was away at a conference in Cambridge until the following day, so Rafferty was forced to hold his desire to interview him in check.

Still, they had plenty of other things to be going on with, as Superintendent Bradley, who bearded Rafferty in his office for an update on the investigation five minutes after his return, was quick to tell him.

'There are a lot more suspects for you to question, Rafferty. What about the landlord of the pub? He could have slipped out the back way and waylaid Sutherland in the car park. I'm sure he must have a fine selection of sharp knives in his kitchen. Have you questioned him further?'

'Not yet, sir. He's on the list. Though as he doesn't appear to have a motive...'

'He's got a wife, hasn't he? You said the victim was a serial philanderer. Strong's wife is an attractive woman. I know, I've seen her. It was the victim's local, you said?'

Rafferty nodded.

'There you are then. The woman was nice and handy. Sutherland must at least have tried it on with her.'

Rafferty was quick to agree to question the landlord, Andy Strong, again, if only to get Bradley out of his hair so he could go and find Tom Kendall and see what he could find out about the electrical warehouse jobs.

But Bradley lingered, questioning Rafferty on what he'd so far accomplished and implying that it wasn't much. Bradley wasn't so much a leader of men as a booter-up-the-backside sort of boss. He hoarded his words of praise and dished them out frugally as if he suspected they were so much gold and not to be wasted on the poor. Rafferty had often wondered if he was as stinting with praise with his children.

But Bradley eventually left, leaving a

fuming Rafferty and plentiful criticism in his wake. After giving his bruised ego a quick buff, Rafferty went to find Kendall.

He found him in the canteen. It was busy, but fortunately, as he preferred as few people as possible to know of his interest in the case, Kendall was sitting at a table on his own. Rafferty brought his tea and his chicken curry over to Kendall's table, said hello and sat down. 'I hear you've got a suspect for the warehouse jobs. Has he squealed yet?'

Tom pulled a face. 'Not so's you'd notice. But he's an old hand and knows how to keep his mouth shut.'

Rafferty, with what he suspected, was glad to hear this response. However, he wasn't so glad to hear what Tom said next.

'Peter Perkins is a dead loss. But I've high hopes of the two youths I suspect of being his accomplices. Inside jobs, I reckon these were. Perkins knew too much about the firms' security for it to be otherwise. And the two scallywags he teamed up with have a bit of form between them. Not very bright, either. I reckon they'll talk once we get our hands on them.'

'Any idea who the fence was?' Rafferty asked, desperate for more information.

'Yeah. Perkins's brother, Paul. Works down the market. Has an electrical stall. You know what a den of iniquity that place is. Reckon the brother's been selling on to favoured customers under the counter. Another brother, Fred, runs a pub, The Rising Sun, by the market, so he, too, had plenty of opportunity to offload the merchandise.' Tom glanced sharply at him as if suddenly curious about Rafferty's questions. 'Why are you so interested? I'd have thought you had enough on your plate with the murder investigation without troubling yourself with my case.'

'Just professional interest, that's all,' Rafferty said with what he hoped was airy nonchalance as he started to tuck into his curry. 'I always like to keep on top of the crop of local lowlifes and their doings. Never know when they might pop up in another investigation.

'Besides, there might be a connection to my case. The victim was a partner in an electrical warehouse business, though not one of the ones that have been turned over.'

'Was he now? What's the name of the firm?'

'SuperElect. Out off the bypass on the business park.'

'Thanks for the tip. Maybe they're next on Perkins's and Co.'s list of places to do over.'

'Always happy to share information, Tom, you know that.' A famished Rafferty had made short work of his lunch. Now, attempting to curry favour so as to wheedle more information out of his colleague, he asked, 'Can I get you another tea?'

'No thanks. I've got to get back to finding Perkins's accomplices and question them before I run out of time on Perkins. I don't want him doing a vanishing act if I have to let him go.'

Rafferty sat brooding after Kendall had left him. He could only hope Tom had no luck in finding Perkins's accomplices if they were likely to lead him further down the line of purchasers of the stolen goods. Because he wasn't altogether sure that his ma wasn't one of them.

The murder team had worked hard and every possible witness and potential suspect – apart from the still-missing Derek Fowler – had been questioned at least once, including those who had argued with Sutherland who were on the list that Andy Strong had supplied. Luckily, most had alibis that stood up to questioning. Of those that couldn't be reliably corroborated – Sutherland's mistress, his son and daughter, the business partner Derek Fowler, not to mention the victim's widow – Rafferty knew he must box clever. Any one of them could have known or guessed that with Sutherland's reputation for upsetting people, he was only too likely to turn up uninvited to his son's stag night. Any one of them could have waited in the car park for him to reappear. They would all have had no difficulty in recognizing his car, an ostentatious silver Jaguar, so would know he must eventually come out.

Having questioned Andy Strong, the landlord, again, as per Superintendent Bradley's instructions, Rafferty had learned that Keith Sutherland had been drinking steadily in the small snug for an hour before he'd entered the main bar and got into the row with his son. And he hadn't been alone, according to the landlord. He'd been with another man, but, though Andy Strong had said he'd seen the man before, he knew nothing about him, not even his first name. Certainly, so far, this man had failed to come forward.

Of the other possible suspects – the superintendent's favourite, Andy Strong, and Sutherland's several ex-friends, who each had only a wife to vouch for their whereabouts – none seemed to Rafferty to have much in the way of a motive, or at least none that they had so far discovered. The landlord must be used to men coming on to his wife. It was one of the hazards of the trade, so Rafferty doubted he'd think the ageing Lothario's efforts in that direction worth any worry.

Rafferty leaned back in his chair and glanced at the clock. Another day was almost over. They had several suspects to check out further, but apart from that they didn't seem to be making much headway.

But, he reminded himself, tomorrow was another day.

'You might as well get off home, Dafyd,' he told Llewellyn. 'Hopefully Sutherland's partner, Derek Fowler, will have surfaced by tomorrow and we can question him.' He hesitated, then rushed on. 'About next Sunday. What if Abra gets cold feet and doesn't turn up?'

'Don't worry, Joseph. She'll turn up. Maureen and I have agreed to collect her. She'll be there.'

Rafferty nodded. He could only hope Llewellyn was right. He'd built himself up for the meeting and it would be a major blow if it came to nothing. But as with the murder case and the electrical warehouse jobs, he'd just have to bear his soul in patience. Worrying about one or all of them wouldn't make things go his way.

Rather than go home, Rafferty headed to his ma's house after work. He was still concerned that she had bought one of the stolen electrical items. She had worked at the local market for a number of years before her retirement and knew all the stallholders, so could easily put herself in the way of stolen goods. She had done so in the past. Rafferty had been unable to cure her of it.

His ma welcomed him, as she always did, with offers of food. He was reluctant to accept her hospitality given what he wanted to talk to her about, but she pressed him and he thought, What the hell. He had little enough by way of food at his own home. Besides, he was hungry. Soon, he had four thick crusty-bread sausage sandwiches in front of him and a mug of strong, sweet tea at his elbow. He pretty swiftly worked his way through the sandwiches and sat back replete.

He studied his ma over his mug of tea as she sat on the other side of the fire placidly knitting a jumper for her granddaughter Gemma's little boy, Joey, her first great-grandchild, and thought what a picture of innocence she looked. But it was a deceptive picture, as he knew.

The thought spurred him on. 'Ma. Remember the wedding present you bought me and Abra?'

She gazed at him over her glasses. 'Of course I remember. I'm not quite in my dotage yet.'

'Where did you get it?'

Ma resumed her knitting, the click of her needles steady. 'Why do you want to know?'

'Because one of my colleagues has a suspect in custody whom he thinks guilty of that series of electrical warehouse thefts.'

'And what's that to do with me?'

'I don't know, Ma. But if it does have something to do with you, will you tell me? It's not as if you don't have some previous in buying stolen goods. Was the gift you bought for our wedding hot?'

'Hot? What strange expressions you use, Joseph. No, of course it wasn't hot. I bought it off a friend of mine.'

'That friend wouldn't be a man called Paul Perkins, would it? Has an electrical stall down the market.'

Ma put her knitting down and stared at him, her lips pursed. 'Just because a man works down the market doesn't make his goods hookey, you know.'

'I know. But I have it on good authority that these goods are. And if – when – my colleague picks up Perkins's brother's accomplices, the whole tale will come tumbling out. I don't want you incriminated, Ma. So, whatever you've got, I'd advise you to get rid of it.'

'I might as well now,' she told him sharply. 'Seeing as it doesn't appear likely that you and Abra are going to make it to the altar.

Not that I need to get rid of it for any other reason.'

'No. Of course not. I'm glad to hear it.' He didn't tell her that he and Abra were due to meet with the hope of patching up their differences. There was no point in both of them getting their hopes up.

SEVEN

When he reached his flat several hours later, Rafferty scrabbled around in his freezer for some minutes before unearthing a beef casserole ready-meal that was past its sell-by date. He shrugged, put it in the microwave, poured himself a glass of Jameson's and, once he'd finished his dinner – straight out of the container – and put the cutlery in the dishwasher, he set to thinking, spurred on by the excuse he'd supplied to DI Tom Kendall for his interest in the warehouse thefts.

Was it merely a coincidence that Keith Sutherland had been a partner in a wholesale electrical company? Or was there some connection between the warehouse thefts and Sutherland's murder? Had he and his partner been scheduled to be the next victims of Perkins and his cohorts?

And, if so, would it have been a put-up job? How would that tie in with Sutherland's murder? Had he been a partner in crime with Peter Perkins?

His business hadn't been going well. His mistress, Carol Mumford, had said as much. Presumably that meant the stock had been moving slowly and money was getting tight. An insurance scam would bring in some ready cash. So, of course, would the agreement to the takeover that Keith Sutherland's business partner had been so keen on. But Sutherland, of course, had vetoed that. Would he have been persuaded to agree to the takeover as Derek Fowler had implied? Or would he have dug his heels in and prevented his partner's comfortable retirement?

Rafferty sipped his drink, swishing the mellow liquid around his gums, then swallowing with a satisfied sigh. Was he thinking along the right lines? If he was, it could mean they were in a different ball park when it came to suspects. Had Sutherland and his business partner both been in on this scam, if scam there was, or just one of them?

If it had just been Sutherland and – for whatever reason – he had tried to back out of the arrangement, things could have turned nasty. And although Peter Perkins had no history of violence, his brother, Paul, had. He'd checked. Paul Perkins had a conviction for ABH. From there, it was but a small step to murder.

Rafferty poured himself another drink. He would be interested to get Llewellyn's take on the scam possibility. It would certainly bear some looking into. How would they have arranged it? And where? Would Peter Perkins or his brother have come to Sutherland's home to arrange the details? It seemed unlikely. His wife would be there and they wouldn't want to risk her overhearing their plans.

Fred Perkins's pub on the other hand, would allow the necessary privacy. It seemed the likeliest location for a meeting. And how would Keith Sutherland have hooked up with the brothers? Had he known them previously? Or had he put a few feelers out?

He'd have to get a recent photo of her husband from Mary Sutherland and get the team to flash it around Fred Perkins's pub, The Rising Sun, and see if anyone recognized him. If they did, it would be a pointer that his thinking was along the right lines.

With that thought to provide sweet dreams, he put his glass in the dishwasher and went to bed.

Rafferty spent a quiet Sunday. Conscious

that clean shirts and underclothes were getting seriously low, he did his laundry and tidied the flat. Then, work done for the morning, he took himself down to The Railway Arms for a quiet drink.

He ordered a pint of Adnams and settled at the bar. The pub was busy; it always was at Sunday lunchtime as the men escaped from the wife and kids to talk football. But this Sunday, football wasn't all they talked. The murder was still a popular subject for conversation and Rafferty earwigged shamelessly on the group of men beside him at the bar in the hope that he might learn something new.

'I reckon the son did it,' opined one. 'Stands to reason. He'd just had an argument with his dad and minutes later the old man's dead. Open-and-shut case if you ask me.'

'Maybe a bit *too* open and shut,' said another. 'Could be an opportunistic killing with the murderer seeing his chance for the son to get the blame and taking that chance.'

'What? He'd come out armed with a blade just on the off chance? Not very likely, is it?'

'The same applies to the son, though, don't you think?'

'I did hear,' said the first man as he lowered his voice so Rafferty had to strain to hear, 'that the dead man made several heavy passes at Andy's missus. And that Andy had already warned him off twice. Maybe he thought that a third time required stronger measures?'

'Not that strong. Andy wouldn't knife him. He's ex-army, remember. Can kill with his bare hands, Andy. I know. He told me one night when we were having a late session.'

'Not likely to do that, though, was he? When he would be the first one the fingers would point at.'

'Shh,' one of the others warned. 'Andy's coming back.'

They quickly switched their conversation back to Saturday's football as the landlord appeared from the saloon bar and Rafferty took the opportunity to order another pint and paid for a carvery meal. Once he'd got his food, he sat down at a table: there was no point in listening in any longer to the men's conversation as Andy remained in the public bar.

He was surprised that the landlord had gone so far as to warn Keith Sutherland off. Had he come on that strong to Vivienne? Andy generally took men flirting with his wife in good part. As he'd said to Bradley, it was par for the course in the pub trade. So what had caused him to go further with

99

Sutherland? Maybe he'd try to have a quiet talk with Vivienne and see if he couldn't find out.

But for now he concentrated on his meal. The lamb was tender and the roast potatoes crispy on the outside and fluffy on the inside, just the way he liked them. He decided against a pudding and sat quietly drinking his beer for another half-hour before he made for home, walking rather than taking a cab as the day was fine.

By Monday morning, the weather had changed. It was wet and blustery and as soon as Rafferty opened the bedroom curtains and saw the rain, the optimism of Saturday drained out of him and he became convinced that he'd made too much of the possible connection between Keith Sutherland's murder and the warehouse thefts. He had always had a tendency to run ahead of the facts. Llewellyn, with his cool logic, acted as a good guard against the tendency. At least, though, he could put his thoughts to the Welshman and see what he made of them.

He jumped in the shower, then dressed quickly, anxious now to speak to Llewellyn and get his take on the theory. He found his raincoat at the bottom of the pile of coats and jackets on the coat hooks by the front door and dropped the rest in a heap on the floor. He'd sort them out later. He looked for his umbrella, but then he remembered it had been broken during his last case, twisted inside out by contrary winds and he'd never got around to replacing it. It was the sort of thing Abra would have done for him.

He shrugged, threw on his raincoat and left the flat, running through the rain to his car. It was a stop-start journey to the station; the rain had brought the town's car owners out in droves along with the usual road-clogging school-run mums. He tapped his fingers on the steering wheel and scowled at the traffic. But he had no choice other than to keep his impatience in check. He turned on the radio to distract himself and was just in time to catch the weather forecast. A low depression had settled over the south of the country and looked set to remain for the rest of the week. He flipped the radio off again in disgust and resumed his finger tapping.

But eventually he made it to the station. Llewellyn, as usual, was there before him. He'd even got tea from the canteen as if suspecting that Rafferty would be in an ill-humour and was trying to assuage it.

Rafferty's bad mood immediately evaporated, especially when he saw that Llewellyn had also purchased some small packets of

Jaffa Cakes.

'What would I do without you, Daff?' he asked as he opened a packet and crammed a whole Jaffa Cake in his mouth. 'Every whim catered for. You're better than a wife. Though don't, for God's sake, tell Abra I said that.'

Llewellyn smiled. 'I've always been a believer in starting the day in the right frame of mind. A good start helps the rest of the day go smoothly. Or, to adapt from one of Syrus's maxims: *vincit qui se vincit*. First learn to overcome our own bad habits. Alternatively: He conquers twice who conquers himself.'

'Good old Syrus. On the ball again. What would we do without those wiseacres?' Rafferty picked up his mug and took a long slurp. Perfect. Strong builders' tea, just as he liked it.

'By the way,' said Llewellyn. 'I rang Derek Fowler's wife and learned that he's now returned from his business trip. I made an appointment for us to see him at eleven o'clock.'

'Good man. I'm even more interested in questioning him now than I was earlier.' Rafferty explained his theory about there being a possible connection between Sutherland's death and the warehouse thefts. He waited anxiously to hear Llewellyn's opinion.

Llewellyn, never one to rush in after fools, took his time in considering the theory. Then he slowly nodded. 'It's certainly a possibility. I'll send one of the team over to Mrs Sutherland's home to get a recent photograph of her husband. We'll know we're on to something if any of Fred Perkins's customers at The Rising Sun recognize Sutherland. It's not as if Perkins's pub is likely to be one of Keith Sutherland's regular haunts. It's not close to either his home or his office. There are, I believe, about half a dozen pubs that are more convenient for either.'

'That's what I thought. So if Sutherland was seen in there it must have been for reasons other than an urgent need for a stiff drink.'

The time till their appointment passed surprisingly quickly. It was 10.45 when they left the station and made for Derek Fowler's home. The Fowlers lived in a detached three-storey house to the south-west of Elmhurst. Like Keith Sutherland's house, the Fowlers' also was looking run-down and in need of money being spent on it. Another indication that, for both couples, money was tighter than it had once been.

Mrs Fowler let them in. She wore an anxious air as she ushered them up to Fowler's study at the top of the house. The inside, like the outside, was in sore need of some redecoration, with wallpaper faded and torn in places.

Derek Fowler was a large, well-fleshed man, who looked as if he would be jovial. But perhaps money worries had knocked any tendency to joviality out of him for his expression became grim as they introduced themselves.

His thinning white hair threw his high colour into sharp relief. The man looked a candidate for a stroke or a coronary, Rafferty thought.

It seemed his wife thought so, too, for she hovered once she had knocked on the study door and let them in, her pale-blue eyes darting worriedly from her husband to the policemen and back again.

Her anxious solicitude seemed to get on her husband's nerves, for he said, with a degree of sharpness, 'You can leave us alone, Doreen. I'm sure they don't bite.'

His wife didn't look as certain of this as Fowler seemed to be because it took another thirty seconds for her to reluctantly leave the room and shut the door behind her.

'Sorry about that.' Derek Fowler gestured to a small settee positioned against the far wall and sat down behind his desk. 'Sit down. I'm just catching up on some paperwork. I've been away at a trade conference.' He paused, then said, 'This visit, I take it, is to do with my partner's recent death?'

Rafferty nodded. 'You heard about it then?'

'My wife told me when I rang home.' He paused, then added, 'I understand he died on Thursday night?'

Rafferty nodded again.

'I was away, as I said. In Cambridge. I left Elmhurst on the Wednesday morning and was away for two days. Terrible business. I must go and see Mary Sutherland and offer my condolences.'

Fowler had been quick to get his alibi in, Rafferty noted. Guilty conscience, he wondered, or a sensible precaution? 'I gather you and the late Mr Sutherland have been partners for twenty years or so?'

'Yes. We both had our own businesses. We met at the local Rotary Club, decided we could do better amalgamating than staying solo and joined forces in 1988. It was a good move, saved us both a lot of overheads.'

'And now, sir? Is the business still doing well?'

Fowler took a few seconds to respond, as if he was weighing what they might have already found out with the possibility of getting away with a lie. However, he plumped for the truth, or at least one version of it.

'Business could be better. I don't deny it. The economy's on a downturn. The banks aren't so keen to lend since the trouble with the sub-prime market in the States. But we were ticking over, ready for the upturn when it came.'

'I see. I'm given to understand that you and Mr Sutherland had an offer from a larger concern that is interested in buying you out. Is it true that Mr Sutherland wasn't keen on accepting their offer?'

Fowler gave a harsh laugh that was meant to sound jovial, but he seemed to be out of practice with joviality because it came out sounding more choked than jolly. 'You have been doing your homework, Inspector. Though you shouldn't believe everything you hear. It's not quite that black and white. Keith could be something of a dog in the manger. But I'd have talked him round to the deal. It was a good one. One we would have been foolish to pass up and Keith knew that. We could have both retired in comfort.'

'But I've been told Mr Sutherland wasn't interested in retiring.'

'He wouldn't have had to retire. Not completely. I'm sure we could have wangled him a part-time executive position with the takeover firm.'

'Some sinecure with little power or responsibility?'

'Not necessarily.' Derek Fowler's voice was sharp as if he feared Rafferty was getting to the nub of the matter. 'Keith had plenty of experience to offer. He'd been in the same trade virtually all his life. Not everybody values only youth and enthusiasm. Keith knew the trade inside out and had plenty of useful contacts.'

If so, they hadn't been much use to him if the business was failing, was Rafferty's thought, though it was one that he didn't voice. 'Tell me about the structure of Super-Elect, sir. You hadn't launched the firm on the stock exchange, I take it?'

'No. We were both private family concerns built up over many years when we joined up. We stayed that way. We were a partnership.'

'And how was that partnership defined?'

'What do you mean?' Fowler shifted in his seat as if he didn't much like the direction the conversation was taking.

'What I mean is – what happens to Keith Sutherland's share of the business? Now he's dead, does it go to his family?'

'Er ... No.'

'What then?'

'We had a form of gentleman's agreement when we first amalgamated, which we later made formal via solicitors. It was because we were both used to being captains of our own ships, you see, and didn't want any control to go to a third party. And then we're both gambling men. Everything falling on the one throw of the dice.'

'So, what are you saying exactly?'

Fowler cleared his throat and with a reluctance that was evident, told them, 'We had an agreement, Keith and I, that in the event of the death of one of us, the other would inherit the entirety of the business.'

'So, with Mr Sutherland's death you now own the whole of SuperElect?'

'Just so.'

EIGHT

Derek Fowler had appeared matter-of-fact about the partnership details and the agreement that now made him sole owner of SuperElect. But it had been a matter-of-factness that he had been obliged to adopt given his timely inheritance of Sutherland's half of the business. But, by his very brief explanation, he seemed, to Rafferty, to have been making an attempt to gloss over the facts, to make them seem unimportant rather than a perfect motive for murder.

Fowler had told them that he didn't know

whether Sutherland's widow or his children had been aware of the details of their partnership agreement. But, he had added, on the whole, he thought not, thereby ensuring that Rafferty was aware that he might not be presumed to be the only party to expect to gain by Sutherland's sudden demise.

'A pretty-cool customer,' was Rafferty's comment as they left the large property after Fowler's still-twittery wife showed them out. 'Must now be looking forward to concluding the takeover, taking retirement and improving his golf handicap.'

'Certainly, to some, prizes worth killing for.'

'Just what I was thinking. He should be able to swing the deal now that Keith Sutherland's not about to put a spanner in the takeover works.'

Derek Fowler had claimed to be away on Thursday night, the night of Sutherland's murder. Booked into a hotel in Cambridge for the trade conference.

'Check with the hotel, Dafyd. See whether he did a disappearing act on the Thursday evening. He could easily have driven back to Elmhurst in order to kill Sutherland. It wouldn't be too difficult for him to guess where Sutherland was likely to be, I shouldn't think. Maybe Sutherland even told him his intentions. He's certainly got one hell of a motive.'

Llewellyn nodded, turned the key in the ignition and pointed the car towards the station. The journey didn't take long.

'The next thing to do,' said Rafferty as Llewellyn parked up in the station yard, 'once we've got this interview typed up and checked out, is to speak again to Mary Sutherland, Susie and Ian Sutherland and see if they *did* know about the terms of the partnership agreement with Fowler. Though, I suppose, given the circumstances, they'll all swear they were aware of it.'

'We also shouldn't forget to look into the possibility that this killing was the work of a mugger,' Llewellyn reminded him. 'I've taken the liberty of asking a couple of the team to concentrate on that angle – look into the local criminals with convictions for robbery with violence. They're currently checking alibis.'

'Yes, of course. You're right. Good thinking, Dafyd. It would be unwise to neglect that possibility. Superintendent Bradley will certainly expect us to check it out as a matter of course, so I want to be able to tell him we've got it covered.'

Good job, he thought, that Llewellyn had put it in hand because doing so had passed *him* by. But he was still convinced that

Sutherland had been killed by someone known to him rather than by a murderous stranger. The act itself seemed to be so calculated, so brutally determined, that he felt strongly that there was a personal element to the attack.

Time and hopefully the investigation itself would prove him right. Meanwhile, he had to plough on with questioning the other suspects. To this end, once they'd got on top of the latest paperwork, he and Llewellyn returned to the Sutherland home to speak to Mary Sutherland.

She was dressed and downstairs when Lizzie Green, back on duty as the shift Family Liaison Officer, opened the door and let them in.

'Any confidences from the widow?' Rafferty asked.

Lizzie shook her head. 'No. Mrs Sutherland is very quiet, very subdued. Her daughter's just left. She's gone home to get some clean clothes and toilet articles. She said she wouldn't be long.'

Rafferty nodded and moved towards the closed living-room door. He knocked and opened it to find Mary Sutherland sitting on one of the three settees. She was staring into space and seemed unaware of their arrival.

'Mrs Sutherland?' Rafferty said quietly so

111

as not to startle her. 'How are you feeling? Has the doctor been again?'

She shook her head. 'He left me some tablets. I'm all right. My daughter will be back soon. She's been very good.'

'I'm sure. She must be a great comfort to you. Your son's been to see you?'

'Yes. He came Friday afternoon and was here all over the weekend. He's been very good, too. I'm a lucky woman.'

Lucky? When her husband had just been violently murdered? Strange point of view, was Rafferty's thought. But he supposed she just meant that she was fortunate in the way that her children were rallying round and helping her to get through what must be an awful time in her life.

He sat down on the edge of the settee facing her and said, 'We've been speaking to Derek Fowler, your husband's business partner.'

'Oh, yes? I suppose he'll be able to retire now. My son has never shown any interest in the business. I think that's partly why Keith refused to retire.'

'Mrs Sutherland, there's something I need to ask you. Something I learned from Mr Fowler.'

She looked blankly at him.

Receiving no encouragement, Rafferty continued anyway. 'Mr Fowler told us that

112

the business partnership was set up in such a way that in the event of one of the partners dying, the surviving partner would own the entire firm. Were you aware of this? Were your son and daughter aware of it?'

She didn't answer immediately. Rafferty knew that shock could slow down a person's reactions, so he waited patiently. Eventually, she answered.

'Yes,' she said. 'We were all aware of the terms of the partnership. Keith made no secret of it. In fact, he used to taunt Ian with it, telling him that if he'd ever shown the slightest interest in the business, he would have insisted on changing the agreement. So my children have no inheritance to speak of, only the house, when I've gone.'

Was she telling the truth? Rafferty wondered. Or had she seen the trap and sidestepped it? Was she simply doing her best to protect her son and daughter from a policeman's natural suspicions?

There seemed no way to prove or disprove it either way. The subject was naturally one that would only have been discussed in the privacy of their family. How could they possibly find out the truth of the matter now? If Mary Sutherland had lied, it was a simple matter, once they had gone, for her to contact her children and bring them up to speed so they didn't contradict her when questioned and put themselves under more serious suspicion. But, if they had known about the partnership agreement they would also know that their father's death would bring them no personal inheritance so their motives for murder would be drastically reduced.

They spent another five minutes with her, commiserating on her loss and bringing her up to date on how the investigation was progressing. They were just about to leave when Susie Sutherland returned. She began to question them in a spikily suspicious way, with questions which Rafferty answered as best he could.

Now was the time to question Susie about the business partnership agreement – before her mother had a chance to prompt her as to her response.

Rafferty asked her the same question that he had asked her mother, but before she could reply, Mary Sutherland broke in.

'I've already told you, Inspector, that both Susie and Ian were aware that, according to the terms of the business agreement, they would only inherit their father's business if Derek Fowler predeceased him. Why do you need to question my daughter about money and inheritances at a time like this? It's very insensitive.'

Stymied from getting an unprompted

114

answer Rafferty sat, grim-faced as Susie replied, 'Yes, I knew about the business agreement. Ian and I both did. It was no secret. We were neither of us interested in the business, so why should we want to inherit it?'

It was a disingenuous response and one that failed to address the fact that, even if it *was* failing, the business would still be worth a tidy sum and would have been an inheritance worth having. The stock alone, even at reduced prices for a quick sale, would have been valuable. And, according to the Land Registry, the partnership had owned the freehold of the property.

But it was academic now. There was nothing else they were likely to learn, so they said their goodbyes and left.

It was one o'clock. 'Let's get some lunch,' Rafferty said. 'We'll try what gastronomic delights Fred Perkins at The Rising Sun can offer us.'

The two-man team Rafferty had assigned to showing Keith Sutherland's photograph around Perkins's bar had met with no success. Rafferty had a twin of the picture in his wallet and he decided he might as well see if he had more luck.

The weather was still rainy and traffic slow. Rafferty watched raindrops slide down the side window as Llewellyn drove, placing bets with himself as to which would get to the bottom first. He lost. It was that kind of day.

The Rising Sun was a small, gloomy, one-roomed pub with a run-down, seedy air. The barmaid was a teenager whose whole demeanour described the phrase 'Abandon hope all ye who enter here'. Certainly, with her stringy, bleached blonde hair, her dead-looking and sludgy grey eyes and pallid face, she looked like she'd abandoned hope some time ago.

'Yeah?' she asked listlessly. 'What can I get yer?'

'I'll have a pint of Adnams and my friend will have a sparkling mineral water. Do you do food?'

'No. No call for it.'

Rafferty wasn't surprised. The bar had a grimy air; he didn't imagine the kitchen was a pan-scrubbed exhibit of the fussy chef's art. Definitely a place to court a dodgy stomach: not something to be risked as he doubted the toilets were up to much either.

'We'll stop off for a sandwich on the way back,' he told Llewellyn as they picked up their glasses and found a table.

The bar was mostly empty, apart from a smattering of market stallholders in the far corner. Paul Perkins, whom Rafferty knew by sight, wasn't amongst them. He strolled over, pulling Keith Sutherland's photo from his wallet as he went. 'Afternoon gents. Detective Inspector Rafferty. I wonder if you could help me?'

An air of suppressed panic invaded the group of five men. They looked furtively at one another as if asking – What have *you* done? What have *I* done?

'Nothing to worry about,' Rafferty reassured them without noticeable success. 'It's concerning a murder that occurred over at The Railway Arms on Thursday night.'

'I heard about that,' one of the men volunteered, a lookalike to Big Ron of *EastEnders*.

'Yes. It's received a lot of coverage locally. We're trying to track the victim's recent movements.' He handed the photo to Big Ron and added, 'I wondered if you'd seen him in here at all.'

Big Ron pursed his lips and stroked his beard as he stared at the photo. Then he shook his head and handed it to the skinny man to his right, who looked, shook his head and passed the photo on. It wasn't until the photo reached a fresh-faced lad surely not old enough to be drinking alcohol that Rafferty struck lucky.

'Yes,' said the lad. 'I saw him. He was in here around a week ago talking to Paul's brother, Pete. They seemed as thick as thieves.'

Possibly because they were, thought Rafferty. 'Paul and Peter who?' he queried, anxious to get his facts straight.

'Perkins. Brothers of Fred the landlord.'

The others, during this discourse, had been trying unsuccessfully and surreptitiously to get the boy to shut up. Eventually, one of them must have given him a terrific crack in the shin under the table, for the boy gasped, bent over and said no more. But he'd said enough. They had their connection to the Perkins brothers. Well satisfied, Rafferty smiled his thanks and strolled back to their table. He and Llewellyn finished their drinks and left.

'We didn't get that boy's name,' Llewellyn remarked.

'Doesn't matter. He clearly works down the market. We've only to ask one of the other stallholders and we'll get his name if we need it. But there's no rush. Park up a minute and I'll get those sandwiches. What do you want?'

'But it's a double yellow line,' Llewellyn protested.

'Don't see any traffic wardens, do you? Do as I say and park up, I won't be a minute. You do want to eat, I take it?'

Llewellyn made no more demurs. Rafferty

climbed out of the car and darted into the baker's. He came out bearing a couple of packs of sandwiches, one of which he tossed in Llewellyn's lap. 'I got you tuna. I know how fond you are of brain food.'

To Rafferty's amusement, Llewellyn hurried to remove the car from the yellow peril. It was the fastest he'd ever seen his sergeant move a car.

'We've got evidence to connect Keith Sutherland to the Perkins brothers,' Rafferty said. 'Maybe now we should set about obtaining a photo of Derek Fowler and see if we can't find out if he and Sutherland were in cahoots in setting up an insurance scam.'

'And how are you going to do that?' Llewellyn asked as he pulled up at the traffic lights.

'Even I've heard of telephoto lenses. I can get a snap of Fowler without him being any the wiser. Maybe the young gabby lad with the bruised shin will remember him too.'

'I would think by now he's been persuaded to keep quiet about anything else he knows.'

'Mmm. I don't doubt his market buddies have marked his card. But maybe the waywardness of youth will persuade him to go his own way. I can but try.'

Llewellyn's Fitipaldi-like removal of the

car from the yellow line turned out to be a one-off and the drive back to the station proved as slow as the outward journey had been. When they got back, they ate their sandwiches at their desks while Rafferty wrote up his report and Llewellyn went through the latest statements.

'Anything?' Rafferty asked once he'd finished his report on the information gained at The Rising Sun.

Llewellyn shook his head. 'Much ado about nothing for most of them, plus the usual outlandish claims from the more imaginative members of the public.'

'Care in the Community has a lot to answer for.'

Llewellyn picked up an envelope and slit it open. 'Forensic report from the car park of The Railway Arms,' he said. He quickly perused the typed lines. 'Nothing of any significance found. Only the usual cigarette butts, crisp packets and other rubbish. No weapon.'

'Didn't think there would be,' said Rafferty. 'I expect whoever killed Sutherland arrived and left by car, so any trace of our killer – cigarette butts, discarded tissues etc. will have remained in the car rather than left at the scene for our opportune retrieval. I reckon our killer waited in his vehicle for Sutherland to stagger back to his car,

120

stabbed him as he was hunting through his pockets to find his keys and left as soon as he'd done the deed. Gives us precious little to go on.'

'Beyond the known facts about Sutherland's behaviour and known peccadilloes.'

'Yes, in spite of what Carol Mumford said about Sutherland's waning libido, his womanizing ways certainly give us a few possibilities. We should be glad of them. Otherwise we might be reduced to just looking for a stray mugger who found a victim who was an easy target. As it is, this case seems more complicated than that. Apart from his womanizing, the peculiarity of the partnership inheritance makes for complications. We can't be sure whether or not Mrs Sutherland and her son and daughter knew of the partnership agreement. On the one hand, if they knew they wouldn't inherit, what would have been the point of killing him, if money was the motive? On the other hand, if they didn't know that Derek Fowler would get the lot, they had everything to play – and kill – for.'

'We ought to investigate whether there was anything else for them to inherit. The house, for instance, and whether it was owned outright or whether it had a large mortgage on it. Then Mr Sutherland might have had savings, stocks and shares, life insurance.'

'We'd need to ask Mrs Sutherland if we can go through her husband's papers.'

'Mmm. It'll be interesting if she agrees.'

'Even more interesting if she makes difficulties.'

But when they visited Mary Sutherland for the second time that day she made no difficulties at all. She simply led them to a small room behind the dining room, said, 'This is where Keith kept all the household accounts and other paperwork,' and left them to it after unlocking the door.

Most of the basic paperwork was contained in foolscap, lever arch files on shelves to the left of the small desk. Each was marked up with its contents: car insurance, house insurance and so on.

Rafferty checked the stocks and shares file while Llewellyn concentrated on the one marked up as containing life insurance, and while Rafferty found that all the stocks had been cashed in during the last six months, the life insurance was still extant. It was a term insurance, which would have come to a natural end when Keith Sutherland reached the age of seventy. He had died two years shy of that age, so the policy was still in force. It would pay out to his estate the not unwelcome sum of two hundred thousand pounds on Sutherland's death.

'We need to find his will. See exactly who inherits what,' said Rafferty. 'Have you come across one yet?'

'No. We seem to have covered all the lever arch files. Maybe the will's in the desk.'

The desk was locked and there was no key to unlock it that they could see. Rafferty sent Llewellyn to ask Mary Sutherland if she knew where it was and he came back with another bunch of keys and Mrs Sutherland trailing in his wake.

'I'm not sure which key unlocks the desk,' she began.

'Don't worry, Mrs Sutherland,' Llewellyn reassured her. 'We'll find it.'

She nodded and went away again, but was back within seconds and said, 'If you find Keith's will, can you please let me know? Ian said I ought to start applying for probate. Not that I'm sure how to go about it. Perhaps you gentlemen could advise me?'

Llewellyn nodded. 'I'll download some forms for you later today. I imagine your husband's computer is password protected so I can't do it here.'

'I've no idea. I have nothing to do with it. Keith always saw to all our household paperwork, you see.'

'Do you have a solicitor, Mrs Sutherland?' Llewellyn asked.

'Keith had one for the business. I don't

know whether he just deals in business matters or whether he deals with private clients, too.'

'Do you know the name of the firm?'

She named a firm on the High Street.

'I know of them,' Llewellyn told her. 'I'm sure they deal across the range of legal activities, though I'm sure your husband's business partner, Mr Fowler, would be able to advise you.'

'Yes, of course he would. I'm sure he'd be willing to help me, even if he and Keith had—' She broke off and Rafferty finished the sentence – even if he and Keith had had a falling out recently over the takeover issue.

Llewellyn managed to find the correct key to match the desk. Once again Mary Sutherland left them to it. It was extraordinary, thought Rafferty. Almost as if she thought their financial and other records were nothing to do with her. He supposed a lot of wives of her generation were like that. The husband had always dealt with everything, often in a secretive manner, so that the wives were left high and dry and woefully ignorant of their own affairs when left alone. Still, given that Derek Fowler looked set to do very nicely out of the partnership, he would surely be willing to help his late partner's widow in her hour of need.

Llewellyn found Keith Sutherland's copy

of his will in a folder in a hanging file in the bottom right-hand drawer of the desk. It was a simple enough document, with the house and all its contents left to his widow and the life insurance divided three ways with the bulk of the funds going again to the widow. There was a codicil that had been added five years earlier and which left fifteen thousand pounds to Carol Mumford; it now worked out at exactly one thousand for each year that her and Keith's relationship had endured. It wasn't much to show for so many years' sacrifice and devotion on her part. But perhaps she hadn't expected anything at all? Perhaps she had been content to settle for Sutherland's company twice a week or less?

They quickly sorted through the rest of the paperwork in the desk. It mostly consisted of utility bills and bank statements. There seemed to be no savings. Perhaps Keith had plundered them to keep the business afloat? The current bank account showed a four thousand pounds overdraft with a five thousand limit. He'd been living above his means. Strange, given the circumstances, that he should imply that his son's fiancée was some kind of gold digger.

There was a small photocopier on a side table. Rafferty switched it on and got Llewellyn to figure out how it worked so they could copy the will, the life insurance and the latest bank statement. While he was doing that, Rafferty went in search of Mary Sutherland and told her they'd finished in the study and that they'd let her have the paperwork she needed before they left.

She thanked him. 'I've just been on the phone to Derek Fowler,' she told him. 'He said he'd come over this evening and help me to go through the papers.'

'That's good. It's always helpful to have someone with business training to go through such things. I'm sure he'll sort you out and will help you deal with the solicitor and so on. While I'm here, are there any other papers we might need to take a look at?'

She shook her head. 'No. Keith kept them all in his study. He liked everything in one place.'

Rafferty nodded. 'Before we go, Mrs Sutherland, did your husband keep an address book? We didn't find one in the office.'

Mary Sutherland stared at him for a moment, then she nodded. 'It should be here somewhere.' She reached out a hand to the hall telephone table, fumbling under the telephone directories. She found what she was looking for – a slim black book. She handed it over.

Rafferty flipped through it. There were a

lot of names in it. They would all have to be checked out. He thanked her, put the address book in his pocket and told her they'd see themselves out when they had finished and went back to the study. He picked up Llewellyn, who, by now, had finished his photocopying and sent him to hand the relevant papers to Mrs Sutherland before they left, with Llewellyn clutching their own copies of the documentation.

Mary Sutherland gazed forlornly after them as if suddenly conscious that she was to be left alone and didn't want to be. But she said nothing, just stood on the doorstep and watched them as they walked up the path. She was still there when their car disappeared round the corner.

They had learned several useful things. And as Rafferty said, at least the paperwork proved the bereaved family of the murdered Keith had something to inherit. Two hundred grand was a tidy sum and well worth killing an unloved relative for.

NINE

Rafferty was driving home and was approaching The Railway Arms when he saw Andy Strong pull out of the pub car park. On the spur of the moment, he slowed and indicated a left-turn into the pub yard. He was relieved to see that the car park was almost empty. But it was early yet and there were likely to be few customers in the bar. It meant he should be able to speak to Vivienne in relative privacy – if she was there.

She was, alone behind the bar, with no one within earshot. As always, she looked well turned out, in a sleeveless green blouse with more than a hint of cleavage. Her natural red hair was loose and swung freely to her shoulders. Not for the first time, Rafferty thought that Andy Strong was a lucky man. 'Evening, Viv,' he greeted her. 'Quiet in here tonight.'

'That's Mondays for you. It's funny, you'd think the start of the working week would make people keener on a stiff drink, but it's

128

not so. What can I get you?'

'I'll have a pint of Adnams, please. Have one yourself.'

'Thanks, I'll have an orange juice.'

'Andy not about?'

'No. He's gone to see his brother.'

'So how have you been with all the upset the murder must have brought?'

'Bearing up.'

'The man who was murdered was a regular here, I believe?'

'Yes. Was in several times a week. Andy was thinking of barring him.'

'Really? Why's that?'

'He was too fond of causing arguments and unpleasantness. He had a way of ruining the atmosphere. He also made a nuisance of himself among our women customers.'

'I heard tell he tried out his ageing charms on you a few times.'

Viv laughed. Clearly, she hadn't taken Sutherland's attentions seriously or been worried by them. 'Andy had a word. Warned him to stop making a nuisance of himself. Apart from that argument with his son, he'd behaved himself the last few times he was in here.'

'Unusual for Andy not to laugh it off,' Rafferty remarked. 'That's what he usually does when men make a pass at you. I know, I've seen him do it.'

'Perhaps he's just getting a bit more sensitive as he gets older.'

Vivienne was getting on for twenty years younger than Andy who was in his early fifties, so it was understandable if he was beginning to get a bit touchy about other men coming on to his wife.

Several other customers came in then and Viv left him to serve them. He finished his pint quickly, having learned what he had come in for, raised his hand in farewell and left to go home.

The rest of the week passed with insufferable slowness both on the murder and Abra rapprochement fronts. But at least, on the latter, Sunday finally arrived and, with it, Rafferty's meeting with his estranged fiancée.

He spent the morning in an agony of anxiety and indecision. After nicking his chin with the razor and staunching the red flow with spit-dampened toilet paper, he went into his bedroom and stood in front of the wardrobe.

What to wear? Should he dress scruffily and try for the sympathy vote? Or should he dress smart and risk her thinking he was fine on his own? There again, he decided, Abra would be unimpressed if she thought he had made no effort. She'd think it showed he didn't care. She'd never been one to be impressed by self-pity; the oh-poor-me look would only earn her contempt.

Would one of the pricey Italian suits he'd bought just prior to a previous case be too over the top? Or would smart casual be the thing? Torn, he decided to ask the advice of his sartorially decisive sergeant. Luckily Llewellyn was at home and answered the phone.

'It's Sunday,' he said firmly. 'Smart casual would be best, don't you think?'

'I don't know. That's why I'm asking you.'

'Smart casual,' Llewellyn repeated. 'And don't forget to polish your shoes.'

'And wash behind your ears,' Rafferty muttered to himself as he thanked Llewellyn for his advice and put the phone down, feeling like some grunting teen on his first date without the sense to dress himself.

Damn. He'd forgotten to ask Llewellyn if he should buy flowers. He didn't want to risk ringing back and getting Maureen, Llewellyn's wife and Rafferty's sometimes acerbic cousin. Mo would be sure to say something to make him feel even more discomfited than he already felt. Anyway, the only outlet for flowers likely to be open on a Sunday morning was the local petrol station with its tired and fading blooms. What message would they send? Better to turn up empty-handed than to arrive with an inferior gift. He'd spent so long ineffectually deliberating over his choice of attire that he'd left himself with no spare time to go further afield. Perhaps he should buy chocolates? Trouble was, he couldn't remember if Abra preferred milk or plain. Defeated again by indecision, Rafferty came to the conclusion that it might be better to just bring himself rather than turn up with wilting flowers or the wrong sort of chocolates. And in spite of Llewellyn's other advice to leave the alcohol alone, he had a couple of stiff ones before he ordered a taxi. They would settle him, he decided. After all, he didn't want his first meeting after the fallout to go completely Abra's way. It would make a mockery of the stand he'd taken over their wedding arrangements. Conciliatory, but prepared to stand his ground should be his order of play. Willing to meet her halfway, but no further: that was reasonable, he thought. Even Abra at her most intransigent should be willing to see that, even if she came to their meeting in a bullish mood. Mustn't she?

Half fatalistic, half hopeful and fully determined to make their meeting a success, he finished cleaning his teeth for the third time that morning, surveyed himself in the full-length mirror for the umpteenth time and pronounced himself ready. Or as ready as he'd ever be and walked out to the waiting cab.

The taxi driver turned out to be the chatty sort; the last thing he wanted when he needed to concentrate on his lines. Eventually, his muttered, resentful responses must have penetrated the mind of Mr Geniality behind the wheel because the cabbie's setting of the world to rights petered out and in its stead there was a blissful silence. Though Rafferty found it wasn't so blissful at all. At least the cabbie's unreconstructed views had distracted him. Now, with the sound of silence, all he had to listen to was the thump, thump, thump of his own too-fast beating heart and the pell-mell rush of unwelcome doubts. Suppose Abra, in the time since she had left him, had found some big-spending boyfriend who didn't try to stint on wedding plans? Suppose she'd discovered she didn't love him, after all? Suppose—?

He forced his mind to stop its helter-skelter ride to a crash. Calm, Rafferty, that's what you need, he told himself. Calm and dignity. If she thinks you're too eager, she'll have you for breakfast, lunch and dinner.

He began to wish he was back in his flat rather than heading towards a make-or-break meeting with his ex-fiancée that would decide his future. At least such a sadgit existence gave some certainty to life.

But it didn't take long after the taxi driver had dropped his incessant gabble for them to reach their destination. Rafferty, striving to retain what was left of his equilibrium while his heart performed whirligigs, paid off the cab, straightened his jacket, took a deep, calming breath and entered the pub.

Obedient now to Llewellyn's strictures, he went to the bar and ordered himself a mineral water. Then he looked round the bar for Abra, Llewellyn and Maureen. They hadn't arrived yet. Rafferty wondered if he should chance a swift shot of Jameson's to steady him. Then he thought better of it. There was nothing wrong with Abra's sense of smell; even over a blast of breath freshener she'd get a whiff of alcohol. Best to leave it alone. Llewellyn was right. He found a seat close to the door so he could see when they arrived.

Time ticked by. He'd finished his water and thought about getting another one. He'd wait till they got here, he decided. He glanced at his watch. They were late. It wasn't like Llewellyn, but Rafferty could imagine Abra delaying matters just to unnerve him.

It was quarter past one when his mobile

rang. It was Llewellyn and he had bad news.

'Sorry Joseph. Looks like Abra's changed her mind. I can get no answer either at her flat or on her mobile.'

'Is her car there?'

'No. No sign of it. Unless she parked it somewhere other than her usual place. Would you like Maureen and me to come to the pub still?'

'No. Don't worry about it. I appreciate your setting all this up, Dafyd. It's just a shame Abra decided not to show. You get off home and enjoy the rest of your Sunday.'

'What are you going to do?'

Rafferty could hear the concern in the Welshman's voice: it showed in the way that his Welsh accent, mostly educated out of him, became more pronounced when he was feeling stressed. 'Don't worry, Dafyd. I'm not going to stay in the pub and drown my sorrows.' I'll go home and do it, instead, he thought. He said goodbye to Llewellyn, waved to the barman and headed home, deciding the twenty-minute walk would do him good. Maybe he ought to take in a trip to the supermarket on the way and stock up. He was getting low on everything, including booze.

His shopping was done in less than an hour, his ready meals for one and his alcohol no longer at critical mass. He'd even thought to buy some bleach for the bathroom and might even remember to use it.

He rang for a taxi on his mobile and was soon headed home. He quickly stashed his shopping, then slumped full length on one of the new settees, a glass with a generous measure of Jameson's clutched in his hand.

He wondered what Abra was playing at. Had she been serious when she'd agreed to meet him? Or was she just toying with him?

He didn't know and he didn't intend to spend the rest of the day brooding about it. He'd phone one of his brothers and see if they wanted to take in the latest Bruce Willis film, maybe go out for a drink after. That way, if Abra should happen to drive past, she'd see that she wasn't the only one able to go out and enjoy herself.

Mickey was at home and was happy to take in a film. He agreed to pick Rafferty up and when he turned up half an hour before the film was due to start, he was in a teasing mood.

'You must be at a loose end, Joe, to ring me up for an outing.'

'Yes, well. You know how it is.'

'Abra still playing it cool?'

Rafferty nodded, but said nothing further. He was thankful Mickey knew nothing about the abortive meeting Llewellyn had arranged with Abra. He'd never hear the end of it if his brother knew. 'Come on,' he said. 'Let's go. We don't want to miss the start.'

Mickey grinned, but followed Rafferty out the door.

TEN

As Rafferty had anticipated, he woke with a sore head after his night out. And as he gradually came to, a feeling of being hard-done-by also surfaced as he remembered Abra's failure to turn up the previous day. What was she playing at? he wondered. He'd thought their reconciliation was all but in the bag. Now he didn't know what to think.

As soon as he got up, in order to cure the hangover, he drank a pint of water and swallowed some painkillers. Still, he thought, as he headed for the shower, he and Mickey had had a good time the previous night. The film had been action-packed all through and afterwards they'd bumped into some mutual friends in the pub. He'd had to take some joshing about his single state, but it had all been good-natured and he'd shrugged it off

137

with a few wisecracks of his own. He should make a point of going out with Mickey more often. Perhaps he and Abra had got too bound up with each other, too insular, it wasn't healthy.

Out of the shower, feeling better than he had first thing, he dressed and made himself some breakfast, forcing it down with a pint-mug of tea. Then, set up for the day ahead, he made for the station and whatever awaited him there.

However, he wasn't prepared for the discovery that what awaited him was another murder.

'Any connection to our current case?' he asked Llewellyn as soon as the Welshman had told him the news.

'It seems possible, seeing as our murder victim is Carol Mumford, Keith Sutherland's mistress. Though uniformed seem to think it possible it's a burglary gone wrong.'

'Bit too much of a coincidence for my liking. Who found her?'

'One of her neighbours. Noticed the lock was smashed and the front door ajar when she passed at eight forty-five this morning on her way to work.'

'OK. We'd better get over there. How was she killed?' he asked as they left the office and headed for the scene.

'Beaten round the head with the prover-

138

bial blunt instrument.'

'Back of the head or the front?'

'Back.'

'So it seems likely she knew her killer and trusted them enough to turn her back. Maybe the lock was broken after the event to make it look like a burglary. Anything missing? Place trashed?'

Llewellyn unlocked the car and they both got in. Once he was settled behind the wheel, Llewellyn said, 'Uniformed say the living room and bedrooms were both in disarray, but it looked superficial, so maybe you're right and it was made to look like a burglary.'

The Scene of Crime team was drawing up as they arrived at Carol Mumford's block of flats. Rafferty said a few hellos, got into his protective gear and followed them up in the lift.

He saw the damaged lock, splinters of wood on the floor, inside and out, then he entered the flat. The body lay in the hallway on its front, with the head towards the living-room door.

It seemed that he was right and Carol Mumford *had* known her killer and had felt no qualms about turning her back on whoever this person was. They'd checked out her background as part of the investigation into Keith Sutherland's murder. Carol

Mumford worked as a personal assistant to one of the executives of a supermarket chain that had moved its headquarters out of London to Elmhurst a few years ago.

Rafferty had rung them and spoken to her boss and had learned that Carol Mumford was well thought of, with good relationships with the other staff. She had earned a decent salary, so if she had been Sutherland's killer it didn't seem likely that it had been in order to get her hands on the measly fifteen grand he'd left her, even if she'd known about it. But even if she had good relationships with her workmates, it was clear someone had hated her – the wounds to her head, Rafferty saw as he hunkered down by the body, were deep, through to the bone.

It seemed she had been caught unawares and had been entirely unsuspecting of the blow as there were no defence wounds to her hands. There were some bloodstains on the right-hand wall. It looked as if Carol Mumford had staggered and slid down the wall, leaving a trail of blood.

Who could have known Carol Mumford well enough and have reason to hate her, but be unsuspected by her of violent intentions? There surely couldn't be too many suspects, not once they'd spoken to her family and friends.

Rafferty stepped back from the body to allow Lance Edwards, the photographer, to do his work. He went into the living room and looked around. It seemed like uniformed were right. For although bookshelves had been emptied on to the floor and drawers in the bureau pulled out and dumped on the furniture, there seemed to be no attempt made to hunt for valuables as several small silver knick-knacks had been left untouched. He crossed the hall. It was the same in the bedroom. The double bed was made up. A large jewellery box opened, but its contents only scattered across the bed rather than stolen. What thief would leave behind the several expensive rings and other pricey-looking items of jewellery? No. Someone had tried to make this attack out as a burglary that had gone wrong and made a poor job of it. That hinted, to Rafferty, at a rank amateur, rather than someone with criminal experience.

He explained his reasoning to Llewellyn, who had followed him into the bedroom.

Llewellyn nodded. 'I think you're right.'

'I know I am. I want the victim's life gone over with a fine toothcomb. Any tittle-tattle, any antagonisms, I want to know about them.'

Dr Sam Dally arrived then. As soon as the photographer had finished taking the pic-

141

tures and video of the scene, he knelt down in the narrow hall and got to work.

'What do you think, Sam?' Rafferty asked after Sam had been about his business for five minutes.

'What do I think? I think this carpet could do with being an inch thicker. It's playing havoc with my knees.'

'Old age, Sam. It's creeping up on you. But to get back to the victim – can you give me a rough time of death?'

It was now ten in the morning. Sam Dally lived about twenty miles away from Elmhurst and it usually took him some time to get to a local scene. Luckily, this morning, he'd already been on duty at Elmhurst General.

'My rough estimate would be that the woman died between eleven last night and two o'clock this morning.'

Rafferty nodded. 'I take it that the earlier time is more likely?' That would, he thought, make sense. Carol Mumford's bed hadn't been slept in so it indicated an earlier time – late evening rather than the middle of the night. Apart from any other considerations, a woman living alone would be wary enough of a knock on the door at eleven at night, so a two in the morning knock would be unlikely to get an open-door welcome.

But Sam wasn't able to confirm it either

way and Rafferty had to be satisfied with the timescale he'd been given.

The team was already questioning the neighbours, but, so far, as Lizzie Green reported to Rafferty, no one had seen or heard anything, not even when Carol Mumford's front door had been splintered and the lock smashed. But it was early days yet. Ms Mumford's neighbour on one side must have gone out early and would have to be questioned later. Maybe they'd heard something, seen someone and would be able to help them get the time of the attack more accurately.

He left the team still working at the scene. He could do nothing more there but get in the way. He and Llewellyn went back down in the lift and crossed to the car. He had found Carol Mumford's handbag with an address book, which would be useful. They would need to trace her next of kin and any friends who could fill them in on her life. He found Hanks and handed him the address book, telling him to return to the station and make a start ringing the numbers and finding out what he could.

Meanwhile they knew Superintendent Bradley would expect to be brought up to speed, so they also returned to the station. Rafferty found the super in his office.

'I hear there's been another murder,' he

said as soon as Rafferty had knocked and been bidden to enter.

'Yes, sir. And I think they're connected.' He explained his reasons.

Bradley harrumphed a bit and then admitted, 'Could be. Better get over and speak to the grieving widow then, hadn't you? Strikes me she had reasons enough to bash the mistress's brains out.'

'I was just about to, sir.'

'Well, don't let me keep you.'

Gladly, Rafferty left the super's office, rounded up Llewellyn and headed for the Sutherlands' house.

Mary Sutherland was at home, though there was no sign of Susie, her daughter. Rafferty asked where the girl was.

'Susie's setting up her own graphic design company. It's a new venture for her. She had a meeting with the bank this morning and with some potential clients this afternoon. I told her to go rather than cancel. She can't put everything on hold no matter what's happened.'

Rafferty nodded. 'Never mind. It was you I wanted to speak to anyway.'

'Again? I've told you all I can. I don't know what else I can say.'

'This isn't about your husband's murder, Mrs Sutherland. This concerns the murder of a woman named Carol Mumford.' He

144

saw a fleeting recognition of the name flash into her eyes and vanish as quickly. 'Did you know the lady?'

'Know her? No. I don't believe so.'

'Mrs Sutherland, maybe you know already or maybe you don't and if you don't then I'm sorry to be the one to break the news to you, but Carol Mumford was your husband's mistress and had been for the last fifteen years.' He paused, then asked, 'Are you saying you were unaware of the relationship?'

She stared at him for some moments but didn't answer at first. Then she stuttered out, 'Fifteen years? No. You must be mistaken. I would have known.'

'Are you saying you didn't know?'

'No, of course I didn't. I would have done something about it if I had.'

Someone had certainly done something, though whether it was Mary Sutherland or one of her children acting on her behalf or someone else whose identity they had yet to learn, Rafferty couldn't say. He asked her where she had been the previous evening and into the early hours.

She told him, 'I was at home. I've just been widowed, Inspector, in case you've forgotten. I don't feel inclined to go out on the town.'

'You were home all night?'

'Yes. I went to bed early and took one of the sleeping pills my GP gave me. My daughter was here all night, too. You can check with her.'

'I'll do that. Thank you. Sorry for disturbing you.'

'You didn't disturb me. I've only been wandering around the house like a lost soul. I don't seem to know what to do with myself since Keith – since Keith...' She broke off and didn't bother to finish what she had been going to say. Then she said, 'Was there anything else? Only I thought I'd prepare Susie a bit of lunch before she heads off for her afternoon meeting.'

'No. Thank you, Mrs Sutherland. There's nothing else. We'll say good day to you.'

Once back in the car, Rafferty said, 'Either woman could have slipped out once both had gone to bed. It's interesting that Susie Sutherland should be setting up her own business now. She'll need money for that. Handy that her father's so conveniently died.'

'There's still probate to be gone through. That'll take some time,' Llewellyn pointed out.

'Even so, maybe Susie knew she was going to be coming into money sooner rather than later. Makes you think. Especially when you consider that Keith Sutherland seems to have been careless with his keys. I remember on the night of his murder, Mrs Sutherland thought I was her husband ringing the doorbell and shouted to ask if he'd forgotten his keys again. If he'd made a habit of doing so – which would seem to be implied by his wife's question – it would mean that Susie might have had access to his will and the file with his life insurance details.'

'So might his wife and son.'

'True. Any one of them or all of them together could have known they were down to inherit a fair lump of cash from the life insurance even without the business inheritance, if they really were aware that his death lost them any share of that.'

'It's mere supposition, though. We've no proof either way and Ian Sutherland, at least, seems to have an alibi for the night of his father's murder.'

'Mmm. One that I'm not altogether happy with. Alibied by a few drunken friends, most of whom admitted their memory of the night was addled by alcohol. I presume the memory of Gavin Harold could have been similarly addled and probably was. For all we know, they've just claimed Ian Sutherland was with them all the time since leaving the pub out of a feeling of misplaced loyalty. No,' Rafferty said decisively, 'Ian Sutherland is not off the list of suspects yet.

Not by a long chalk.

'Maybe we ought to find out something about their finances?' he said. 'See how each member of the family is situated. For instance, in Susie Sutherland's case – a new business venture eats money. She'd need to pay out for advertising, website design, premises and so on. None of which come cheap. Then there's Ian. Weddings don't come cheap, either. And I should know,' he muttered. 'And given that his father didn't approve of the bride, it's unlikely that Keith volunteered to get a second mortgage on the house to pay for it all.'

'Would either of them kill Carol Mumford, though?' Llewellyn queried. 'I'm presuming you still think both deaths are connected.'

'I do. Don't you?'

'Yes. Too much of a connection between the two for them not to be.'

'That's what I thought. That being the case, we should proceed from there.'

They had previously questioned Susie Sutherland as to her whereabouts at the time of her father's murder: like her mother, she claimed to have been at home alone. And for Carol Mumford's murder her mother said she had been with her at the family home.

'Get the team to check with the Sutherlands' neighbours, Dafyd. We might strike lucky and come upon a mum with a sleepless baby or a pensioner whose arthritis was playing up. *Someone* must have noticed if there was any movement from Susie, her brother or their mother. If so, I want to know about it.'

While the rest of the team were checking out the Sutherlands' neighbours, the two members of the squad assigned to looking into the local muggers had turned up a couple of possibles for Keith Sutherland's robbery and murder: Dwayne Heller and Nick Bolsover. Both had convictions for robbery with violence, both were drug addicts and were known to habitually carry a knife. More to the point, neither had been able to come up with a confirmed alibi for the time of Sutherland's death.

The possibility that one of the pair was the murderer didn't gel with Rafferty's feeling that Sutherland's murder had been a personal thing, but he knew he had to look into the possibility. So he had Timothy Smales and Hanks, who had come up with the two names, bring Heller and Bolsover in for questioning. The two youths were practised criminals and knew their way around the law and the provisions of the Police and Criminal Evidence Act. Both insisted on having a solicitor present during their questioning.

Dwayne Heller was your typical street thug. As well as convictions for robbery with violence, he'd had a couple of convictions for drug dealing – until someone tougher had scared him off.

Heller looked the low-life he was. To make himself look tougher, his hair was aggressively scalped to within an eighth of an inch. It gave him an aura of butch menace, which was clearly the look he desired.

'Hello, Dwayne,' Rafferty greeted him as he entered the interview room that afternoon with Llewellyn hard on his heels. 'Still the tough guy who mugs old ladies for their pensions?'

Dwayne looked discomfited at this accurate description, but said nothing.

'Cat got your tongue? I heard you had quite a powerful chat-up line with the more mature lady. What was it you said to your last victim? Oh yes, "Give me your money, you old bag, or I'll stick you". Your mother must be so proud.'

'Leave my mum out of this.'

Rafferty sat down in the chair across the table from Dwayne while Llewellyn took the seat beside him. 'Why should I?' Rafferty demanded. 'She raised you, after all and must take some of the blame for the way you turned out.' He turned the tape on before Dwayne's solicitor had a chance to complain and did the normal recital of details for the machine. 'I'm glad we're able to have this little chat, Dwayne. It's always nice to renew old acquaintances, don't you think?'

To judge from Dwayne's scowl, he didn't agree.

'Let's get down to cases, shall we? When you spoke to my colleagues, you didn't seem too sure of your whereabouts on the Thursday evening of last week. Now you've had a chance to think about it have you come up with any ideas?'

'Yeah. I was with a mate of mine. We were in the arcade in the town till it shut at eleven.'

'And can anyone but your mate corroborate that? The arcade owner, say?'

'Yeah. He should do. Why don't you ask him?'

'Oh I will, Dwayne. And what was your mate's name?'

'Nick Bolsover.'

Rafferty managed a smile. 'What a coincidence. Mr Bolsover is also currently helping us with our inquiries.'

'He'll be nice and handy for you to ask then, won't he?'

Rafferty didn't bother to bandy any more words with Heller. Instead, he told the tape that the interview was suspended and went and had Nick Bolsover brought to one of the other interview rooms.

Bolsover was a little older and a lot more streetwise than his friend. He even sang the same song. Either they'd concocted the arcade tale out of guilt or they were telling the truth. Much to Rafferty's surprise, the latter turned out to be the case as the arcade owner soon confirmed.

No easy solutions on this one, then, Rafferty told himself, not entirely displeased that this should be so. It would have been too easy if Sutherland's death had been caused by Heller, Bolsover or both. Apart from any other consideration, their involvement would have left the murder of Carol Mumford hanging strangely in the air with no logical connection to Sutherland's death. And Rafferty didn't for a moment believe there was no such connection.

Hanks's trawl through Carol Mumford's address book had produced a sister, a Mrs Linda Cartwright. She lived at Habberstone, four miles to the west of Elmhurst. It was a pleasant twenty-minute drive and at least they didn't have the prospect of breaking the news of Ms Mumford's death as Hanks had already done that.

Linda Cartwright lived in a modern

bungalow. Its front garden was filled with ornaments: a wooden windmill, a wishing well and several statues of the twee variety.

Mrs Cartwright herself turned out to be a grey-haired mumsy figure in a lemon cardigan and grey pleated skirt. She looked a good few years older than Carol.

She led them into the front room, which was furnished with lots of chintz and family photographs – they covered nearly every available wall surface.

Mrs Cartwright, once they were seated, immediately launched into an explanation for the age difference between herself and her late sister. 'Carol was a late baby for my parents. I imagine my mother must have thought she was starting the change when she fell pregnant again. It must have been a shock to them both as my mother was in her late forties and my father in his early fifties. There's fifteen years between Carol and me, so we were never close. I was almost grown up by then, of course, the usual stroppy teen with little interest in babies, particularly my parents' child. I remember I found it hideously embarrassing that they should have another baby at their advanced age. How judgemental the young are. And now poor Carol's gone. So tragic. And you say she was murdered? I can't think who would want to murder Carol. She didn't have any enemies

153

as far as I know. Not that I would necessarily know; as I said, we weren't close and didn't see a lot of each other. I have my family, of course. They all live quite close and I see a lot of them.' This was stated with a complacent smile.

Rafferty got the impression that she had felt rather sorry for her little sister, the childless spinster who, in her opinion, had been a singular failure as a woman.

Rafferty wondered if she'd known about the regular liaisons with Keith Sutherland. He asked her and learned that she had.

'He was only using her, as I told her. She should have had more pride than to be satisfied with the little he offered. I kept urging her to find a man of her own, but she never listened. She was a little headstrong and spoiled, of course, being so much younger than the rest of us. My two elder brothers doted on her and were forever bringing home presents for her. Of course they both live abroad now, Tony in Spain and Jim in France. They retired there. I suppose I'll have to let them know what's happened. Oh dear. What a dreadful thing. Will I ... will I have to identify her?'

'That would be helpful, Mrs Cartwright,' Rafferty told her. 'We'll make sure there's a car to bring you home.' He could see the prospect wasn't pleasing, but with the brothers living abroad there was no one else immediately available to do it.

It seemed she realized that she was inevitably the one who would have to undertake the task, for she rose, found her jacket and her handbag and said she was ready. 'Or as ready as I'll ever be.' She pulled a face and her eyes became moist. 'It's funny, but you don't expect to bury the baby of the family first.' She looked at them. 'Well, shall we get it over with?'

'You wouldn't like someone to come with you?' Llewellyn asked. 'A friend or neighbour? One of your children perhaps?'

She shook her head. 'My children are all at work. I wouldn't like to drag them away for this particular duty.' She led them out to the car and they were soon on their way. The journey didn't take long. Once they had taken her to the mortuary and the body had been wheeled out, Mrs Cartwright identified it with no evident doubt and stood for half a minute contemplating her dead sister with lowered head and sorrowful gaze. Then, with a sigh, she turned away.

They drove her home, questioning her further on the journey. They had asked Mrs Cartwright if she had knowledge of anyone who nursed a grudge against her sister, but she had told them that beyond her relationship with Keith Sutherland, she knew little of her sister's life. She certainly didn't know anyone who would wish to do her serious harm.

All in all, it had been an unproductive hour and a half. It left Rafferty feeling restless, with the urge to do something. But there was only the endless routine of the now double murder inquiry to soothe his restless spirit and that somehow didn't satisfy.

Investigating those in Carol Mumford's address book any more than doing the same with that of Keith Sutherland, wasn't going to set the heart beating wildly. But such routines were an intrinsic part of any investigation. Though he couldn't help feeling they were wasting their time. Someone who knew both Keith Sutherland and Carol Mumford was responsible for the two deaths and all the address book trawling in the world wouldn't give them an answer.

Sam Dally was being his usual tardy self with the PM results on Carol Mumford. Not for nothing was he nicknamed Dilly Dally. When he got back from Linda Cartwright's home, Rafferty rang and chased him up.

'You're not my only customer, you know, Rafferty,' Sam told him testily when he was put through. 'I've got corpses lined up left

156

and right, all awaiting my attention.'

'Yes, but they're not all part of a double murder investigation.'

'A *suspected* double murder investigation, surely? For all the evidence you've got the murders of Sutherland and Mumford are unconnected.'

'I doubt that. I've a feeling in my water.'

'Ever thought it might be a bladder infection?'

'Funny man. You might scoff, Sam, but such feelings have proved to be bang on the nail before. I've no reason to doubt them this time, particularly as the two victims were very close.'

'Ever heard of coincidences?'

'Never liked them. I don't do coincidences. Anyway, enough of this banter, fun though it is. What can you tell me about Carol Mumford?'

'I haven't been able to narrow down the time of death at all. As to the weapon, I'd say it's something rounded like a baseball bat. Right-handed assailant. There were at least half a dozen blows to the victim's head. Determined to kill her whoever it was.'

'Sounds like it. Strange that the two murders were so dissimilar.'

'Another reason to think they're not connected, I would have thought.'

'Not necessarily. I don't think we're dealing with a serial killer here who goes in for the same MO every time. Maybe the different methods were adopted because one victim was drunk and the other sober. Keith Sutherland would have been an easy victim, half-cut and fumbling around in the gloom of the car park as he was. Perhaps the murderer didn't feel as confident that a knife would be an effective weapon in the second attack. Anyway, that's for me to worry about.'

'That it is and pleased I am that that's so. You'll have my written report in due course – not that it'll tell you any more.'

His spoken report hadn't given him much either, Rafferty reflected as he thanked Sam and put the phone down.

He'd have to solve this case the hard way.

ELEVEN

If Derek Fowler, the late Keith Sutherland's business partner, had left his Cambridge hotel in order to murder Sutherland they had been able to find no evidence of it. Neither had they found anyone who was prepared, on being shown the long-lens shot Rafferty had got Lance Edwards to obtain, to identify Fowler as an associate of the Perkins brothers.

So it looked, assuming Rafferty's suspicions were correct, as if Sutherland had been investigating the possibility of organizing a little insurance scam, with the assistance of the Perkins *frères*, on his own.

Whether Sutherland had come to a sticky end because of some sort of thieves' falling out was debatable. And probably unprovable seeing as the Perkins trio conveniently alibied one another.

But if they *had* killed Sutherland where did the murder of Carol Mumford fit in? For them to kill her also made no sense.

Unless he was barking up the wrong tree

with her death and it really had been what it, on the surface, seemed – an amateur burglary gone wrong.

Rafferty shook his head. He still didn't buy that, any more than he bought Keith Sutherland being attacked and knifed by a stranger whatever the crime figures might say about the prevalence of such crime in modern society.

He threw his pen down, leaned back and closed his eyes. He came to a few minutes later to the dulcet tones of Superintendent Bradley saying: 'Well, if this is how you go about solving your murder cases, I'm not surprised the latest two are going nowhere.'

Rafferty jerked his head up. He blinked owlishly. 'I was thinking, sir.'

'Thinking is it? I'd leave the thinking to them as are able for it. Like Llewellyn. You'd do better to get out there and question every suspect again. See if you can't rattle 'em by repetition. Trip them up by their own answers. That's the way, Rafferty. None of them have contradicted themselves yet, I take it?'

'No, sir.'

'They will. Stands to reason one of them must. Not going to make it happen by sitting on your arse snoring. Think on, but.'

With that last piece of gratuitous advice, Bradley banged out of the office.

Rafferty sighed. If only everything in life were as black and white as Bradley saw it, rather than numerous shades of grey.

But there was no getting away from the fact that the investigation into Sutherland's death wasn't going well. In spite of repeated appeals for him to come forward, the man who had been in the snug of The Railway Arms with Sutherland had still not made himself known. Why not? Who was he and what did he have to hide? And what was his connection to Keith Sutherland?

Rafferty had got Andy Strong, the landlord, to work with the police artist on a mug shot of the mystery man, which he'd shown to Keith Sutherland's family and acquaintances, but no one had recognized him. Unless he came forward voluntarily he would remain a mystery. And he didn't like mysteries. Not when they had to do with murder.

What to do next? He glanced at his watch. It was coming up to twelve. Maybe he and Llewellyn should drive back to the Sutherlands' and catch Susie between business engagements? As nothing else suggested itself, he decided on that course.

The weather was a lot cheerier than he was. Bradley's shot about falling asleep on the job had rankled. It was unfair. But that was Bradley all over. Brickbats were one of his specialities. If he ever handed out bouquets the flowers were sure to have greenfly.

He went in search of Llewellyn and they drove through sunlit streets that made everything look shiny and new. Windows sparkled and trees greenly glistened in their new summer clothing. In fact, everything but him seemed to have put its best foot and face forward to greet the sun. The thought made him feel even more glum.

When they reached the Sutherlands' home, Susie was sharply businesslike to match her dark-grey suit.

She was in the kitchen with her mother just finishing what looked like a salad lunch when they arrived. And after Rafferty had explained the reason for their visit, she asked cuttingly, 'Why would I want to murder a woman I didn't know? Never mind creep out of the house in the wee small hours to do it? The idea's mad.' And so are *you*, her expression implied.

'What time did you and your mother go to bed?' Rafferty asked.

Susie gave a theatrical sigh. 'Mum went up about half nine. Isn't that right, Mum?' She turned to her mother and Mary Sutherland nodded. 'And I went about an hour later. Neither of us sneaked out of the house to murder a woman we'd never heard of. Why would we?'

Rafferty didn't answer her question. Instead, he posed one of his own. 'Are you sure you or your mother didn't know her?' He glanced over at Mrs Sutherland, who shook her head.

'No, of course I didn't know her,' Susie replied. She frowned. 'And this woman was supposed to be my father's mistress, right?'

'Long-term mistress, yes.'

'Dad was no spring chicken. I would have thought any tendency to being a Lothario was long since over.'

'Perhaps it was. Maybe they were more into companionship. But there's no doubt they were close friends of long standing.'

'Well, I didn't know about it as I told you. Mum didn't either. Did you, Mum?'

Mary Sutherland shook her head again.

Rafferty nodded. 'Well, thank you for your time, Ms Sutherland, Mrs Sutherland.' He made to go, then turned back. 'I hear congratulations are in order.'

Susie's eyes narrowed. 'Congratulations? What do you mean?'

'Your mother told us you're starting your own business. A brave move in the current financial climate.'

'That's just the way things have panned out. I'd rather not have tried to get a business off the ground either in the current climate or in the midst of a murder investigation into my father's death. But sometimes the timing of events is out of kilter. It was the right time for *me*, which is the most important thing.'

'I'm sure you're right.' He gestured to Llewellyn. They made their goodbyes and left the house.

'Mary Sutherland was quiet while we interviewed her daughter,' Rafferty commented. In truth, the older woman hadn't spoken one word once she'd let them in. Scared she'd let some scrawny feline out of the bag? he wondered.

'She seemed distracted,' said Llewellyn. 'As if she was hardly in the same room. Of course, she has lost her husband and just learned about his long-term mistress.'

'I don't buy that,' Rafferty scoffed. 'All those years and we're meant to believe she had no inkling? How likely is that? *Someone* would have seen Sutherland and his floozie together and tipped her the wink. If the affair had only been on the go for fifteen weeks, then maybe I could believe she didn't know about it. But not for fifteen years. Some helpful soul would have thought it their duty to break the happy news.

'Besides, I was watching her when I mentioned Carol Mumford's name. She knew her all right. I'd stake my pension on it.'

Llewellyn zapped the car to unlock the doors and they got in. 'What now?' he enquired. 'Do you want to speak to Ian Sutherland again? Find out if he's got an alibi for last night?'

'Sounds good to me. He'll be at work. It might rattle him if we beard him at his place of work.'

This wasn't something that Rafferty normally liked to do, but this case was getting to him: maybe he'd achieve better results if, like Superintendent Bradley, he played the heavy-footed plod.

Ian Sutherland's place of work was a town-centre estate agency. It was an independent and Sutherland was the sole proprietor. Rafferty wondered if he knew his cousin, Nigel Blythe, as they were both in the same line. Maybe he should ask Nigel what he knew of Sutherland?

There again, would it be fair to put the suggestion that Sutherland was a murder suspect into the mind of Nigel, his presumed business rival? On the other hand, all was fair in love and murder as he was sure Nigel would put it.

Ian Sutherland wasn't very welcoming when they were shown into his office.

'You again,' he said with a scowl. 'What do you want now? I'm just on my way out to meet a client. And I don't appreciate your coming to my place of business.'

'And there was me thinking you'd be glad to help find your father's murderer,' said Rafferty. This earned him another scowl.

'Well, you're not going to find him here.' Sutherland glanced at his watch – a showy timepiece that seemed to have more dials than Concorde. 'I can give you five minutes.'

Rafferty smiled. 'Good of you. I doubt it will take that long. All we need to know is where you were last night between the hours of eleven p.m. and two a.m.'

Ian Sutherland's gaze swivelled between the two policemen. He looked rattled – like a man with no alibi would look rattled. 'Last night? Why? What happened last night?'

'If you've got an alibi you don't need to be concerned, do you, sir?' Rafferty quietly remarked. 'So where were you? At home? Out with your fiancée?'

Sutherland seized on the last suggestion like a man going down for the third time. 'Yes. That's right. I was with Georgie, my fiancée. Georgie Green. We were at my flat. I cooked dinner. I drove her home around midnight.'

Curious how Sutherland had covered the most important hour of those that he had mentioned. In spite of Sam Dally's implacable refusal to shorten the presumed time of death from the three hours between eleven and two, Rafferty, from the evidence of the still-made-up bed at Carol Mumford's home, had shortened the most likely timelines for himself. He had glanced in Sutherland's kitchen when they had visited him on the morning after his father had died. It had looked decidedly underused – no grease staining the cooker and no dirty utensils littering the worktops. In fact, the only evidence of the culinary arts that the kitchen had evidenced had been the pile of takeaway fast-food containers escaping from the swing bin. The idea of Sutherland actually cooking a meal for his fiancée struck Rafferty as as unlikely as himself cooking the Rafferty clan Christmas dinner. He doubted this particular young man could cook more than a boiled egg.

But, unless his fiancée insisted on telling the truth, it seemed to Rafferty that he had been the agent of his own misfortune. Me and my big mouth, he thought. Why did I put the idea of the alibied night spent with his future wife into Sutherland's brain? It had been stupid and his own stupidity annoyed him mightily. But there was nothing to be done about it now, not unless Sutherland's fiancée turned out to be a young lady with a mind of her own. And Ian Sutherland didn't strike him as the sort of man who would appreciate a woman with a brain and the willingness to use it.

Rafferty, still annoyed with himself, just asked for the fiancée's address and phone number and left an Ian Sutherland who was clearly itching to reach for his mobile and get alibi back-up.

'I made a mess of that, didn't I?' he said ruefully to Llewellyn once they were back in the car.

'You did, rather,' Llewellyn agreed.

'Don't hold back,' Rafferty snapped. 'Just tell it like it is, why don't you?'

'I thought I just did,' Llewellyn replied mildly. 'I suppose it depends on whether he's telling the truth. Or whether his fiancée is a good liar. Either way, unless he was seen on the street and we find out, we've hamstrung ourselves.'

'*I've* hamstrung us, you mean. Stupid of me. I don't know why I put an alibi in his mouth. It's not like me.'

'But you're not like you at the moment, are you? Not with this business with Abra still hanging over you. Let me see if I can get hold of her this evening. Then you might not suggest alibis to suspects.'

Rafferty nodded sombrely. 'You're right. I'm out of sorts so Sutherland got an Abra-alibi. Stupid of me,' he said again.

'Well, it's done now. The only thing is to

speak to this Georgie Green. See what she says. She may not back him up if he's lying.'

'She's going to marry him, isn't she? She's bound to stick up for him. Why wouldn't she? She won't want the suspicion of murder hanging over her would-be husband's head – not with the wedding only a few weeks away.'

'Let's wait and see. You want to visit her at home this evening?'

Rafferty nodded. He'd forgotten to get the young woman's work address. 'Yes. It'll give her a few hours to get rattled if she's contemplating lying to us. We'll go and see Nigel Blythe, see what he can tell us about Ian Sutherland and then get back to base. See if anything new has come in.' He wasn't hopeful.

Rafferty was lucky and he and Llewellyn caught Nigel in his office.

The estate agency was quiet with few customers in the outer office. Of course there was a downturn in the economy and estate agents like Nigel were suffering accordingly. Banks and building societies had cut back on their mortgage business and unless you had a hefty deposit your chances of getting a mortgage were slim.

Whether Nigel was suffering financially, he looked as smart as ever, today in a lightweight mauve suit with a lemon shirt and tie. But then Nigel always looked debonair as if he had his own personal valet on tap. It was one of the more irritating things about him.

'Well, if it isn't my copper cousin and his oppo,' he greeted them as they stood in the doorway. 'And to what do I owe this pleasure?'

'We're looking to pick your brains, Nigel,' Rafferty told him. 'About Ian Sutherland, one of your competitors.'

'Why? What's he done?'

'Nothing that we can prove. It was his father that was murdered in The Railway Arms. You might have read about it.'

'It was *that* Sutherland, was it?'

Rafferty nodded. 'Did you know the victim?'

'I think I met him once or twice in one of the local pubs. Can't say I took to him.'

'What about his son? What can you tell us about him?'

'Not a lot. Only that I heard his business is having a worse time of it in the current climate than most.'

'Any tendency to violence?'

'Not to my knowledge. Can't hold his drink though – I've socialized with him at several estate agents' conventions and he has a tendency to get belligerent with booze.

170

Why? Are you thinking of removing him from circulation? Think he did for his old man?'

'He's one of a number of suspects, that's all. We've nothing else against him. You said his business wasn't going well. Think he's on the brink of going under?' It would mean Ian Sutherland was under even more financial pressure, which would be an added reason for him to kill his father for his inheritance.

'Could be. I make a regular study of the competition and have a few willing spies in place – you're not the only one with informants, coz. His business has been going downhill rapidly. The properties he's got on his books haven't been moving. Most have remained unsold for months. He must be getting desperate.'

Desperate enough to kill? Rafferty wondered as they thanked Nigel for his information and left the agency. Ian Sutherland had been on the spot at the time of his father's murder and, given his financial difficulties, certainly had one hell of a motive. A motive exacerbated, according to Nigel, by his business being on the brink of disaster. Ian Sutherland must have been getting increasingly desperate as the weeks went by with no lucrative sales. People had killed with much less reason.

★ ★ ★

Much to Rafferty's surprise, something new, something *helpful*, had come in during his and Llewellyn's absence.

A young woman stood up when they entered reception and moved towards him at Bill Beard's nod. 'Inspector Rafferty?' she asked.

Rafferty nodded and she introduced herself. 'My name's Georgie Green.'

Rafferty felt wrong-footed. What was Ian's fiancée doing here? In his mind, he'd relegated the interview with her to this evening. 'What can I do for you, Ms Green?' he asked, stalling for thinking time.

She gave a faint smile. It softened her somewhat hard features. 'I think it's more a case of what I can do for you, actually. You know I'm Ian Sutherland's fiancée?'

Rafferty nodded.

'Ian rung me a short while ago. Wanted me to lie for him. I wouldn't do it. I *couldn't* do it. I was with a gaggle of girlfriends last night, at least two of whom have very loose tongues and one of whom is going out with a policeman. They'd break his alibi in a moment if they were questioned. What's the point? As I explained to Ian.' Her lips turned down. 'He didn't take it very well.'

'I appreciate your honesty, Ms Green,' Rafferty told her. 'Not everyone would be so frank in the circumstances.'

'It would have been stupid to agree to Ian's demands, particularly when a few questions would have disclosed the lie. And so I told him. He wasn't very pleased.' Her face puckered for a moment and Rafferty thought she was going to cry. But she was obviously made of stern stuff and managed to hold the tears at bay.

Rafferty was surprised that Ian Sutherland had chosen to marry such a strong-minded young woman. Maybe there was more to Sutherland than he had suspected? 'Come up to my office,' he invited. 'And we can talk. Does Mr Sutherland know you're here?'

She shrugged as he pressed the door code and ushered her through and up the stairs. 'I imagine he can guess. He might have been stupid to try such a lie, especially with me. And you,' she added generously with a little sideways smile. 'But he's not generally lacking in perception.'

Once seated in Rafferty's office, he asked her if she knew where her fiancé had been the previous night.

'He told me he'd been at home all night. He said he had an early viewing this morning so wanted a quiet night.'

'And did you believe him?'

'Yes.' She met his gaze squarely. 'Yes, I did.

173

Ian's not normally a liar. I wouldn't be marrying him if he was. I'm not a complete fool. But this business with his father's murder has seriously rattled him. He's all at sixes and sevens, particularly as his alibi for it rests on a few drunken friends.'

'Do you think he had anything to do with his father's death?'

She shook her head vehemently. 'Ian hasn't got it in him to kill anybody, least of all his father. Ian and he might not have got on as well as they could have, but he was in awe of his father and his business ability. You know he started the business before Super-Elect from scratch?'

Rafferty shook his head. 'Ian didn't resent his father? Resent what he'd achieved? The fact that he hadn't left his share of the business to Ian and his sister?'

'No. Not at all. You're on the wrong track, Inspector, if you think he had anything to do with his father's death. Nothing could be further from the truth, believe me.'

Rafferty would like to. Even if only to remove one suspect from the list. But whatever Georgie Green said, it was still early days yet and he wasn't willing to cross anyone's name off the list.

TWELVE

'Right,' said Rafferty, once Llewellyn had escorted Georgie Green back to reception and returned. 'I suppose we ought to check what Derek Fowler was doing last night. Just because we haven't been able to find a sign of him leaving Cambridge on the evening of Keith Sutherland's murder, doesn't mean he couldn't have caught a train to get back to Elmhurst in order to kill him.'

'True. But can you think of any reason why he should wish to kill Carol Mumford?' Llewellyn asked.

'No. Dammit, of course I can't. Must you always ask such impossible questions?'

'Asking impossible questions forms part of the usual murder investigation. Or it did when I was trained. If it comes to that, what was there to stop *Mrs* Fowler doing the deed? She, at least, was on the spot, with as much, monetarily, to gain as her husband.'

'Doreen Fowler? She struck me as too much of a nervous Nelly to commit murder.'

'Maybe that's why she's so nervous. Guilty conscience.'

'But we don't even know if she was aware that the business partnership agreement would benefit her and her husband in the event of Sutherland's death. Mind, perhaps we should ask her? And there's no time like the present. Come on. We can have lunch when we've questioned her.'

It was another pleasant drive, the day still being fine. Derek Fowler was, of course, at work, but his wife was at home.

Doreen Fowler was, as Rafferty had said, a nervy woman, though he couldn't make up his mind whether that was her natural state or whether it was their presence in her home that brought on the condition.

She let them in with the breathless information that her husband wasn't at home, as though she couldn't imagine the circumstances where anyone might want to speak to *her*. She led them into the living room and invited them to be seated. It was a spacious room, over-fussy and just as Rafferty had imagined a nervy woman like Doreen Fowler would furnish her home. There was too much of everything: too many little tables scattered over the orange flowered carpet, its pattern clashing with those of the pink and cream easy chairs. The pictures on the walls were bland landscapes with no fire or colour. Rafferty wondered how anyone could deliberately design a room with such a clashing colour scheme and such dreary, colourless pictures.

Doreen Fowler clothed herself in as dressy a way as she furnished her home; flowery top, flowery skirt, even flowery earrings in the form of small yellow-centered daisy studs. None of which matched each other. Much like the house.

Rafferty wondered if she was colour blind. It was usually a male affliction, but some women did suffer from it. It would explain a lot. Unless she was a woman of little taste or discernment.

'Do you want me to ring my husband and fetch him home so you can speak to him?' she asked anxiously, her hands massaging each other against her stomach.

'No, no. That won't be necessary,' Rafferty assured her. 'We can catch him at work. It's about last night we wanted to speak to you both about.'

'Last night? We were both at home last night. You can ask Derek. He'll tell you the same.'

Rafferty was sure he would once his wife had rung him. He noted how quick she was to provide this information. Was that evidence of guilt or a peculiarly naive guilelessness?

'Why do you ask, anyway? What's happened?' She stared at him in breathless anticipation.

He found Doreen Fowler an irritating woman – he wondered how her husband could stand living with her. Rather brutally, he said, 'Another murder's happened, that's what,' not bothering to dress it up.

'Another—? Oh dear. That's dreadful.'

Strange, Rafferty thought, that she failed to ask who had been murdered. Maybe there was more beneath Doreen Fowler's nervous exterior than he had thought. 'Don't you want to know who died?' he asked.

She blushed hotly as if she'd committed some social solecism, then stuttered, 'Yes. Yes, of course. If you want to tell me.'

'It was a Ms Carol Mumford. I gather she was Keith Sutherland's long-term mistress.'

'Really? How dreadful. Poor woman.' Then, as an afterthought, she added, 'Poor Mary. How very distressing for her.'

'Were you aware of the relationship?' Rafferty asked.

'Well ... em ... no ... em ... well ... em, I think I had ... em ... heard something. From my husband, you know.'

'Yes, of course. Did you know Ms Mumford? Had you ever met her?'

'Em ... er ... No. I don't believe so. That is,

well hardly. Not the done thing to flaunt a mistress, is it?'

'Was Keith Sutherland the flaunting type?'

'Well, no. That is to say, really, I can't be expected to know. It's my husband you should be talking to. We didn't socialize with Mary and Keith. Not often, anyway. It's not as if he'd bring his mistress, this Carol Mumford, along to family events, is it? Though –' she screwed up her face – 'I believe Derek pointed her out to me once.'

'Tell me, Mrs Fowler, were you aware that your husband and Keith Sutherland had a mutually beneficial business partnership?'

'Mutually beneficial?' she repeated as she looked vacantly at him. 'What do you mean?'

Rafferty explained.

'I believe Derek mentioned something of the sort once. I didn't really take it in. Most of Derek's business dealings go over my head.' She gave an embarrassed laugh. 'I'm afraid I'm not really into all the business ins and outs.'

Could anyone really be so disingenuous? Rafferty wondered. Mrs Fowler was in her sixties: could anyone go through so many years of life in such ignorance of her husband's business and its gain or otherwise to herself?

But, currently, there was no answer to that

179

question, nor did one – beyond her denial – look likely to be forthcoming just yet. Maybe her husband would be more enlightening.

But Derek Fowler, when they presented themselves at his office at the SuperElect premises, in between irritatingly interrupting business phone calls, simply repeated the same information that his wife had given them: namely, that both had been at home on the previous evening and that he believed he might have mentioned to his wife that the entire business would revert to him should Keith Sutherland die, but he wasn't sure that she would have retained the information.

The two interviews had been pretty unsatisfactory from their point of view. Rafferty hoped that wasn't going to turn out to be par for the course.

Rafferty left for home that evening, feeling despondent at his lack of progress. As he drove to his flat, he reflected again that he didn't seem to be getting very far in the investigation for all the interviews and reports that kept piling up on his desk. He parked in his designated parking place and went up to his flat. As he shut the front door behind him the silence seemed to echo resoundingly. That and the loneliness seemed to have physical entities. He didn't know how much longer he could stand it. It wasn't as if he could go out on the lash with Mickey every night and still do his job.

To break the oppressive sound of silence, he noisily dropped his keys in the bowl on the hall table under the mirror. But the silence, when the jangling sound of the keys had died away, seemed worse than before. He shrugged out of his jacket and went into the kitchen to put his solitary meal in the microwave. He put the kettle on and stood gazing desultorily out of the window while he waited for it to boil.

The house phone rang and he went to answer it. It was Llewellyn. 'You just caught me. I've only now got home.'

'I've managed to get hold of Abra,' Llewellyn told Rafferty after the usual greetings.

'And?' Rafferty asked eagerly. 'Did she—?'

'She got cold feet about the meeting. She feels badly about it and didn't know how to make amends.'

'A phone call would have done.'

'I think she knows that, at heart. Now, she wants me to arrange another meeting.'

'Will she turn up for this one?' asked the once bitten, twice shy, Rafferty.

'I believe so. I suggested the meeting takes place at my flat either with Maureen and me as mediators or without us. Maureen and I can make ourselves scarce if you prefer.'

'Let's see how it goes,' said Rafferty, scared that Abra might take flight if Mo and Llewellyn abandoned her. 'When does she want to meet?'

'Tomorrow evening. Eight o'clock.'

'That soon?' Rafferty did his best not to read too much into it.

'I think she's scared to allow herself too much time to think about it. Possibly that was the trouble last time.'

'Suits me. Thanks, Dafyd. Thanks for persevering. I'm sure it's a pretty thankless task you've taken on.'

'Oh, I don't know. I'll be delighted if I can help resolve your problems. You haven't exactly been Mr Joyful since the split, you know. I'd like to get back the old Joseph.'

So would I, thought Rafferty as he bid Llewellyn goodbye and put the phone down. The flat no longer seemed so silent as, whistling, Rafferty went back to his tea-making.

The next day, Rafferty was up early. He had only had a couple of celebratory glasses of Jameson's after speaking to Llewellyn and his head was clear, his thoughts upbeat. He looked forward to the meeting with Abra that evening as he got ready for work.

The drive to the station was trouble free.

The sun was still shining. All was right with the world. It made Rafferty nervous, but when he arrived at work there was nothing awaiting him to give him palpitations. Even Superintendent Bradley wouldn't be breathing down his neck, as, according to the grapevine, he was away from the station for the entire day.

'So, what have we got, Daff? Anything new and juicy come in? Any more murders?'

'No. We've still only got the two.'

'Thank God for that. These two are giving me enough trouble. Let's have a run through with where we are on both.'

They spent the rest of the morning discussing the two investigations – what they'd done so far and what remained to be done. Llewellyn took notes.

'We haven't spent much time checking out Keith Sutherland's ex-friends,' Rafferty remarked towards the end of the session. 'Though, like Derek Fowler, his wife and the Perkins brothers, I can't see what connection they can have to the murder of Carol Mumford.'

'Nor me. But it doesn't mean there isn't one. We could at least get a couple of the team to check their whereabouts during the likely times for Ms Mumford's death.'

Rafferty nodded. 'Do that. It's best to be thorough. I don't want to give Bradley any more of an excuse to find fault.' He paused, looked speculatively at Llewellyn, and said, 'About tonight – are you sure Abra will turn up this time?'

'Yes. I'm sure. She was keen to get the meeting organized as quickly as possible. She's genuinely sorry that she backed out before and knows she's been unfair to you.'

'There's no one else in the picture?'

'No one else?' Llewellyn's brow furrowed.

'I mean she hasn't had another bloke sniffing around?'

'I see. She didn't say. But even if she has, they can't be important. It's you she's asked to meet.'

Rafferty nodded. 'That's true.' He felt better for Llewellyn's reassurance. But now was not the time to dwell on personal matters. Time enough for that this evening.

'Well, let's get on,' he said. 'You get on and arrange for two of the team to question Gilbert Fortescue and Randolph Hurley and I'll get and write up yesterday's interviews. Let me have your notebook, would you?'

Llewellyn handed it over and went out.

The tapes from the CCTV cameras nearest The Railway Arms had all been gone through after Keith Sutherland's murder. The trouble was that none of them had a focus on the car park entrance. Anyone could have slipped in with the camera none the wiser and hidden up to await Sutherland's return to his car. The team had checked out all the car owners whose cars had been driven within a hundred yards of the pub. They'd been questioned and mostly eliminated. A few had merited further investigation, especially those who'd admitted knowing the murder victim, but, so far, nothing had come of the checks. Rafferty didn't hold out much hope that it ever would. He was still convinced that this murder had its source closer to home. He had nothing to back this up; it was still just a feeling, one that had refused to leave him.

He eventually finished typing up Llewellyn's notes. He hated typing. Hated computers. He'd never really got to grips with technology, in spite of the compulsory courses he'd been sent on. Llewellyn had taught him all he felt he needed to know to function in his job. And if he didn't know how to do something, there was always Llewellyn, his own tame computer nerd.

Llewellyn came back and reported on the interviews with Fortescue and Hurley.

'They both say they were at home with their wives at the time of Carol Mumford's murder. Hanks and Lilley questioned the neighbours, too, but they all say they didn't notice either of the men leave their homes. Of course, Carol Mumford didn't die before eleven at night, so several of the neighbours had already gone to bed.'

'Either one of them could still have slipped out. But again, why would they? This second murder is causing us untold problems, isn't it? Every time we come back to a suspect having no apparent reason to kill both victims.' Rafferty ran his hands over his face and head. This action left his unruly auburn hair looking even more untidy. He noticed Llewellyn's amused glance and quickly smoothed it down as well as he could.

'What now?' he asked. 'Any suggestions?'

'We could always try checking the CCTV cameras nearest to our various suspects' homes for the nights of both murders. Something might show up.'

Rafferty pulled a face. 'That'll make me Mr Popularity.' Checking through an eternity of CCTV footage was not the most eagerly anticipated duty with his colleagues. 'But, OK, do it. It might give us something. It's not as if we've got any other leads.'

The rest of the day dragged slowly. They, as yet, had no results from the latest trawl through the CCTV tapes. If their killer had walked and worn a hoodie, they'd be no further forward. None of the suspects' cars had shown up on the footage so far checked; Rafferty didn't hold out much hope that the latest search would be any different. Everyone was wise now to the dangers of CCTV picking them up if they were in the course of a crime. Like Rafferty himself, anyone intent on killing and with an ounce of sense, would leave their car at home and head out to commit their crime on foot and with their faces and bodies covered with suitably anonymous clothing and using back doubles where no cameras lurked, where possible.

The only suspects, so far as they knew, who could have had reason to kill both Keith Sutherland and his mistress were his family. But was that too obvious? Sometimes things were that simple. And after all, most murders were family affairs. And there was no lack of motive for any of the three. Mary Sutherland had jealousy, revenge and financial gain. Her son, Ian, and daughter, Susie, also had financial gain as motives, that good old standby. Also, if they knew about their father's long-term affair with Carol Mumford there would be anger on their mother's behalf. And it had to be said that neither sibling seemed exactly broken-hearted at the loss of their father.

★   ★   ★

The long, unsatisfactory working day finally wound to a close. It couldn't come soon enough for Rafferty; he was never at his best when a case seemed to have turned stale. He preferred plenty of action on an investigation with lots of leads. His brain then seemed to ping from one to another and make connections.

But this case was behind him for the day. Now he had to concentrate on the evening ahead.

THIRTEEN

Rafferty was relieved when he reached Llewellyn and Maureen's flat that evening and was let in, to see that, this time, Abra had actually turned up.

She was sitting in Llewellyn's minimalist living room clutching a large glass of red wine and smoking a cigarette. Rafferty, who had given up the weed some months before, felt like bumming one off her. Always supposing she'd spare him one. Her face looked set and unfriendly as if she were having serious doubts about this meeting. He felt his heart do a back flip at the realization that he might, after all, have lost her for good.

Yet she *had* turned up. Surely that meant something? Like that she still had feelings for him.

He watched as she lit another cigarette and he furtively inhaled the smoke. He was surprised that Llewellyn had allowed her to smoke in his home; he and Maureen were pretty hot on maintaining their no-smoking ban. But the palpable tension in the room explained Llewellyn's unusual relaxation of the rule.

Rafferty drew a deep breath and said, 'Hello, Abra. You're looking well.' She wasn't, as it happened. She looked decidedly rough, but Rafferty didn't feel it a good idea to say so.

'There's no need to play the distant stranger routine, Joe. I'm not looking well at all and I know it. I look like shit.'

As the dark shadows under her eyes and their lacklustre dullness attested to this, Rafferty thought it better to say nothing, but he just managed to catch himself from nodding an agreement with her statement. Abra's long chestnut hair looked dry and lifeless; her nails were bitten to the quick and she had put her make-up on with a shaking hand if the traces of mascara on her eyebrow told him anything. I'm not a detective for nothing, he thought. He was relieved that he wasn't the only one feeling sick to the stomach.

'How have you been?' she asked once she had taken a huge gulp of her wine and another drag on her cigarette.

'Lonely. Missing you.'

'You should have thought of that before.'

'I know.' He hoped this wasn't going to turn out to be all his fault. He tried again. 'What about you? Have you missed me?'

'I've been far too busy to think about missing anyone,' she retorted sharply as if to admit to such a weakness would loosen her game.

'I've been busy too,' he told her. 'You've probably read about my latest murder in the papers.'

'I can't say I have. I've been way too busy at work to read the papers or watch the news.'

This was hopeless. He'd thought she'd at least meet him halfway, but she was barely quarter there. He glanced at Llewellyn for some encouragement.

Llewellyn, who could be a bit of a wuss when it came to emotions, escaped into the kitchen under the pretext of fetching more wine. Instead, Maureen took the ball and ran with it.

'Why don't you tell him the truth, Abra? You know very well you've missed him, too.

You told me so.'

Abra's intransigence slackened a bit at this revelation. 'Well yes, all right then. I suppose I did miss you. But that changes nothing unless you change your views.'

'And what about your views, Abra?' he asked quietly. 'Are they capable of change, too?'

'Yes. I think so.' Suddenly she smiled and it was the old Abra; the warm-hearted girl rather that the chilly-faced bitch. 'I suppose you could say we've been stupid, Joe. *I've* been stupid.'

'That makes two of us. But we don't have to continue being so.'

Llewellyn returned just then from the kitchen where he had discreetly retreated while they got through the first awkward moments of their meeting. He must have been listening for a suitable moment to return. He carried a glass of wine, which he handed to Rafferty who was still standing just inside the door.

'Sit down, Joseph,' said Llewellyn. 'I'll not let Abra bite, don't worry.'

Rafferty gave a strained grin, took the wine and sat at the opposite end of the settee to Abra.

'Dafyd's right,' she said. 'I won't bite.' Strangely playful now the frost had finally thawed. 'Or are you playing hard to get?'

He gave another strained smile and edged over.

'Can Maureen and I safely leave you two to get reacquainted?' Llewellyn asked. 'Or do we need to stand guard in case violence breaks out?'

'No. You get off, Dafyd,' said Rafferty. 'We won't be coming to blows, will we, Abra?'

She shook her head.

'Good. There's more wine in the kitchen if you want it and Maureen made coffee. It might be better in the circumstances if you switch to that once you've finished those glasses. This is a situation that calls for clear heads, don't you think?'

Rafferty and Abra nodded sheepishly.

Llewellyn and Mo left soon after. A silence descended which they both tried to break at the same time.

'After you,' said Rafferty, playing the gentleman.

'I was just going to say it's good to see you again.'

'And you. God, how did we let things degenerate so far?'

'I rather think that was down to me,' Abra admitted. 'I was the one who refused to take your calls or answer the door when you rang. You at least tried.'

As that was true, Rafferty didn't attempt to deny it. 'At least we're talking now,' he offered. 'It's a start. Let's make sure it leads to where we want to be.'

Abra clutched her glass tightly and nodded. 'Dafyd tells me you're in the middle of another murder investigation or rather two murder investigations. How are they going?'

'About as badly as they could be,' Rafferty told her. 'We seem to be stalemated.'

'But that's not unusual, is it? You've had cases before that seemed stuck in a groove.'

'Most of 'em,' Rafferty agreed with a rueful smile.

'But you got there in the end.'

'True. I'll keep that in mind when the current case frustrates me. But this meeting isn't about my work. It's about us. If there still is an "us".'

'There's still an "us" as far as I'm concerned. I've behaved unreasonably. I see that now. I hope I'm big enough to admit that most of the fault's been on my side. I was wantonly extravagant over the wedding. I won't be again, I promise. That is, if you still want to marry me.'

It had clearly taken Abra a lot to admit she'd been at fault. Rafferty felt the least he could do was admit to his own share of the blame.

'Of course I still want to marry you. And I was a tight-fisted git over the wedding arrangements. I'm sorry about that.'

193

'Meet halfway?'

Rafferty nodded. He took Abra's glass and placed it beside his own on the coffee table. 'Can I kiss you now?'

'Don't say you've forgotten Dafyd's "May I?" grammar that he's been at such pains to teach you?'

'Stuff Dafyd and his grammar. Now's not a time for grammar.'

'OK. God, yes, it's been so long.'

Five minutes later, Abra came up for air and said, 'I didn't tell you, but Dafyd and Mo aren't coming home this evening. Dafyd told me the flat was ours for the night if we wanted it. Mo's even made up the double bed in the spare room. I had a peek in earlier. You should see it – all scented candles and perfumed pillows. It looks like a veritable knocking shop.'

Rafferty stood up and took her hand. 'Then let's not waste it,' he said and led her through to the spare room.

Abra was back in his life and it felt good. She was moving back into the flat later today – she still had her key. Rafferty felt elated as he drove home the next morning to change his clothes; he'd even lost his feelings of frustration over his current investigations, though, inevitably, that didn't last beyond his arrival at the station.

Little that was new had come in. And Bradley was on his back again now he knew that Ian Sutherland had no alibi for Carol Mumford's murder.

'Why don't you bring him in?' he had demanded. 'You've reason enough, God knows. What's stopping you?'

'A little matter of proof, sir.'

'Bah. A few hours of questioning and even you might succeed in dragging the necessary proof from him. But OK, have it your own way, though I shall want you to keep me updated on a regular basis.' With that he had stomped off.

The rest of the day had passed in a similarly depressing mode. But it ended at last. Much to Rafferty's delight, Abra had been as good as her word and had moved her clothes and other paraphernalia back into the flat.

The place had a wholly different aura when he got home that night. She'd even cooked and a delicious smell of chicken casserole wafted towards him as he walked down the hall. He glanced in the living room to see she'd taken trouble with the table. The best wine glasses, candles and their linen napkins sat decorating the table-top. A small vase of early roses was placed in the centre.

'The place looks beautiful, sweetheart,'

Rafferty told her, 'and that casserole smells divine.'

'I thought our reunion deserved a bit of effort,' she told him. 'There's pudding courtesy of Marks and Sparks. A lemon soufflé.'

'Sounds great.' Rafferty took his hands from behind his back and presented her with a large bouquet of red roses and a bottle of champagne. He kissed her and said, 'I'll put this in the wine cooler.'

'So,' he said, some minutes later as the kissing had extended rather longer than he had anticipated. 'What do you want to do for the rest of the evening?'

'You, mostly. I've missed you. We've some making up to do.'

'What about the casserole?'

'Stuff the casserole. We can eat it later. I'll turn it down and it'll be fine.' She took him by the hand and led him to the door, blowing out the candles on the way.

Rafferty was full of beans the next morning. He greeted Llewellyn cheerily, wished him 'top of the morning' like some pseudo Irishman. 'By the way, Daff, I wanted to thank you and Mo for giving up your home for the night. It was good of you. And you'll be glad to know it worked – the wedding's back on again.'

196

Llewellyn gave the broadest smile Rafferty had ever seen him give. 'Really?' he asked. 'I'm so pleased. Wait till I tell Maureen.'

'Be a devil and ring her in work time rather than make her wait till this evening.' He picked up the telephone receiver and handed it to Llewellyn. 'Now seems as good a time as any. I'll get the teas and a sticky bun each.' Rafferty headed out the door and left Llewellyn to break the happy news to his wife.

Tea and buns bought, Rafferty settled down to the paperwork with nary a groan. He kept this up for the rest of the day aided only by copious quantities of hot, sweet tea and a sandwich from the canteen. Even the sun had come out to match his upbeat mood and Bradley hadn't come near nor by. All he needed now to make his day complete was for the solution to the two investigations to come to him.

Rafferty had thought it likely that he'd get all three of the Perkins brothers together in Fred's pub on a Thursday evening. And so it proved. The brothers were huddled around the counter, Fred, the landlord, behind the bar and Peter and Paul standing the other side of it when he and Llewellyn entered.

'Evening, gents,' Rafferty greeted them. 'How's the electrical warehouse thieving going? On the up?'

Three stony faces met this remark. At first, none of them said a word, then Fred, with his thin, ferrety face and thinner whiskers, who was clearly the spokesman of the group, in his role as Mine Host, said, 'We can have you for that. Casting aspersions on our good names, that is.'

'The last time you three had good names must have been when you hung from your mum's tit for the final suck before you were weaned. Let's not get hot for the compensation culture, lads. Even if you go with one of those no win, no fee vultures, you'll still have to pay the opposition's costs when you lose.'

Fred scowled. 'What do you want?'

'Nice of you to ask. I'll have a pint of Adnams with a whiskey chaser and my friend will have a mineral water.'

Fred made no move to fulfil the order. He simply stood and stared at Rafferty with a malevolent glare. 'What do you want?' he repeated tonelessly.

'Me? I want to know where you three gents were on the night that a certain Ms Carol Mumford was murdered.'

'Who? Never heard of her? When is she supposed to have been murdered?'

Rafferty told him. 'Going to alibi one another again, are you? Like you did with

Keith Sutherland's death?'

'We didn't kill him. What reason could we have? We didn't even know the man.'

'That's not what I heard. Heard you were as thick as thieves. Planning another warehouse job, were you?'

Fred spluttered indignantly. 'Here, you can't say that.'

'I've just said it.'

'Anyway, we didn't do this Sutherland bloke and we didn't do this latest one. We're not killers, whatever you might think. We were all three here in the back room that night. You can ask my bar staff. Tammy Smith was on duty that night. She's out the back taking her break. I'll get her.' So saying, he quickly disappeared into the grimy bowels of the bar.

He reappeared a few minutes later with the same teenage barmaid who had served Rafferty on his previous visit to the pub. She was inclined to be surly, having been dragged off her break, but she confirmed what Fred Perkins had told him readily enough.

There seemed little more to say. Into the silence, Fred, with a sly look on his face, as if he already knew the answer, asked, 'Rafferty, you said your name was?'

Rafferty nodded warily, wondering where this was going.

'Any relation to Kitty Rafferty? Used to

work down the market.'

His brother, Paul, put in, 'Been a good customer of mine over the years. If you know what I mean.'

Rafferty thought he knew only too well to what he alluded.

'Only, I know she had a brood of kids and your face looks familiar,' Fred went on.

Rafferty was quick to deny being related to his mother. If Paul Perkins *had* sold his ma electrical goods from his market stall, of the stolen variety, he didn't want confirmation of the relationship to give the brothers a lever to use against him. He'd better have another word with ma and make sure she wasn't still housing anything that would incriminate her and damage him.

'It's an unusual name. You and Kitty are the only Raffertys I've come across,' Paul told him. 'Strange you're not related with you both living in the same town and all.'

This conversation wasn't going the way Rafferty would have liked. It was bad enough that his ma bought hookey gear, but for the Perkins brothers to suspect the relationship was altogether a suspicion too far. Thoroughly rattled by now, Rafferty wanted nothing more than to get out of the pub and round to ma's as quickly as possible. But to make his excuses and leave too quickly would surely give them reason to speculate on his hasty departure and conclude that their suspicions about the relationship had been spot on. So he forced himself to question them pointlessly for a further five minutes before he felt he could safely leave.

Just before the door closed behind him and Llewellyn, he heard Fred shout after them, 'By the way, you're barred.'

Rafferty grinned and stuck his head back round the door. 'That's fine by me. If this was the last pub in the town I wouldn't want to drink in it.' For good measure, he slammed the door behind him.

Of course Llewellyn was curious as to why he'd denied half his parentage.

'Why did you deny that Mrs Rafferty is your mother?' he asked as they climbed in the car.

Rafferty thought quickly. 'Those three have a dislike of coppers. Could be they might take that dislike out on ma if they know we're related. Safer to deny we're from the same family.'

Llewellyn looked unconvinced. 'None of them have convictions for revenge attacks and only Paul has a conviction for violence and that was a drunken brawl. It's possible they might have opened up more if you had confirmed the relationship. After all, Paul Perkins said your mother was a customer of his.'

Too good a customer, thought Rafferty. If Paul Perkins had been selling stolen electrical goods on his stall, which seemed likely, there was no knowing how many items in ma's house might be iffy. If one of the three brothers was convicted for the warehouse jobs they might well mention his ma's purchases out of spite. It wouldn't do his career any good for his ma's illicit purchases to come to light.

Dammit, he thought as he walked back up the road to the car, why did his family always seem to cause him grief? Other coppers didn't have a family load weighing them down. Why did such a load have to rest on his shoulders? He remembered their last case when his brother, Mickey, had caused him major angst by getting himself in the frame for murder and now his ma was in danger of being done for being in possession of stolen goods.

He dropped Llewellyn at the station to pick up his car and left him in order to check through the latest reports. His checking was cursory and ten minutes later found him hurrying back to the car park in order to drive to his ma's.

She was at home when Rafferty arrived. After he explained his dilemma, she came across as remarkably complacent.

'You worry too much, son,' she told him after she had made the tea and brought it back to the living room.

'You'll have something to worry about, too, if Paul Perkins drops you in it. If he's done for receiving, do you think he's likely to protect the customers who bought the goods his brother nicked? Especially not if coughing up gets him a reduced sentence. There's no honour amongst thieves, Ma. That's a fallacy.'

'Is anybody – apart from you – saying I bought stolen goods?' When Rafferty didn't reply, she asked again, 'Are they?'

'No,' Rafferty admitted. 'But that's not to say they won't if enough pressure is brought to bear.'

'So why haven't Paul and his brothers been arrested?'

'It's not my case. I don't know for sure, but I imagine the officer in charge is lacking sufficient evidence. The Perkins brothers are smart enough to keep their mouths shut when questioned and deny everything.'

'So you've got nothing on any of them,' his ma stated with an air of being proved right.

Rafferty was forced to admit it and he added, 'We've got our suspicions. Paul and his brothers have been on the police radar for years.'

'Exactly, and with nothing to show for it.

You've just got a downer on him and his brothers. Maybe you should concentrate your efforts on real criminals, violent criminals and leave the likes of the Perkins brothers alone.'

'I came round here for your sake, Ma. If, as I said, Peter Perkins admits to the thefts and Paul to receiving stolen goods, and lets slip the names of some of his customers, you might yet see the inside of a police cell.'

Ma shook her head at this and calmly sipped her tea.

Rafferty admitted defeat for the time being It was clear his ma paid little heed to his warning. He'd just have to hope his colleagues didn't get enough information on the Perkins brothers to charge them.

The next morning, when he reached the station, Rafferty sought out Tom Kendall, the DI in charge of the warehouse thefts investigation. He found him in his first floor office, nearly buried behind piles of paperwork.

'Too busy for a chat, Tom?' Rafferty asked as he entered the office.

'I'm too busy for a crap, Joe. I've been in since seven. You can see how I'm fixed. But,' he threw his pen down and sat back, 'I'm about due for a break. Too much work and all that making Tom a dull boy. What can I do for you?'

'It's about these warehouse thefts. I wondered if you've made any progress?'

'Why?'

'It's just that I'm still concerned about the possibility that there's a connection to my murder case – you know the first victim, Keith Sutherland, was a partner in an electrical warehouse?'

'Yeah, you said. I doubt there's a connection. The Perkins brothers aren't killers.'

'There's always a first time. Criminals have always stepped over the line. And if Sutherland arranged for Peter Perkins to break into his warehouse for an insurance fraud and then changed his mind, it's possible things turned nasty.'

'I told you, the Perkins brothers aren't killers.'

Rafferty decided to try another tack; he was keen to know if Kendall was any nearer to making one or more arrests. 'Did the two youths you suspect of being in cahoots with Peter Perkins spill any beans?'

'No. Nary a one. I reckon one of Perkins's brothers got at them. I'm beginning to think that these thefts are destined to join the unsolved-cases file. Everyone I suspect of involvement has played shtum. Not a word out of anyone.'

'What first put you on to the Perkins

brothers, anyway?'

'One of my snouts. He's usually reliable, but I'm beginning to wonder if he's got his wires crossed on this case. If the Perkins brothers *were* the guilty parties, they're hiding it well. Paul Perkins even let us examine the contents of his lock-up. Not a sign of any stolen goods.'

'Maybe he had time to shift them.'

'Maybe, but where to, we don't know. The trail's gone cold now so unless we get some new evidence it looks like they'll get away with it.'

Rafferty restrained the relieved grin that wanted to spread across his face. 'Bad luck,' he said. 'You win some, you lose some.'

'How are your murder investigations going? I hope you're having better luck than me.'

'Not so's you'd notice. But I'm still hopeful. We've various strands to follow. We're getting there even if it is slowly. Anyway, I'll let you get on.'

Rafferty shut Tom's door behind him and walked, whistling, up the stairs to his own office.

FOURTEEN

'We've got a witness who claims she saw Susie Sutherland near The Railway Arms on the night her father was murdered,' said Llewellyn as he put the phone down.

Rafferty swung his chair back from his contemplation of the weather – it was tipping it down and the leaves of the trees opposite his office dropped forlornly with the weight of water as it dripped from them. 'How positive is this witness?'

'Very. She knows Susie Sutherland well by sight. In fact, she says she only noticed her because Miss Sutherland appeared rather furtive.'

'Furtive? In what way furtive?'

'She was walking along very close in to the hedges and was wearing a headscarf close around her face as if she didn't want to be recognized.'

'Was she indeed? Where's this witness now?'

'She's on her way in. Constable Beard will ring us when she arrives.'

'Depending on how reliable this witness comes across, we may well have to have another word with Susie Sutherland.'

The woman who had seen Susie Sutherland, a Mrs Adams, seemed a sensible woman.

'And you're sure it was Miss Susan Sutherland that you saw near The Railways Arms?' Rafferty questioned again wanting to be sure before he spoke to Susie again.

'Yes. I'm quite sure. I know her pretty well. I used to live down the same road as her and her parents and saw her regularly.'

They had questioned Mrs Adams for twenty minutes and hadn't been able to shake her on her story. It gave Rafferty the confidence to question Miss Sutherland again.

'Give her a bell, will you, Dafyd?' he said after they had taken Mrs Adams's formal statement and shown her out.

Susie Sutherland was inclined to be surly and at first attempted to deny she had been anywhere near The Railway Arms on the night of her father's death.

'You say someone saw me? Who? I've told you, they must be mistaken.'

'No mistake, I don't believe, Miss Sutherland. We have a very positive identification.

You were there. The question is – why?'

For a moment, Rafferty thought she was going to continue to deny it and break out into a tirade of abuse. There were two hectic spots of colour high on her cheekbones, which could have been temper or another overwrought emotion.

But the temper tantrum never evinced itself. Instead, she burst out,

'All right. I was there. So what? I didn't kill him. He was my father, after all.'

'So why were you there? On the spot?' Rafferty asked again.

'I wanted to get my father on his own and ask him for a loan. Just until my business gets established.'

'And did you speak to him?'

'Oh yes. I spoke to him all right.'

'And? Did he agree to the loan?'

'No. He laughed at me. Told me to go to the bank as he'd had to do when he started up.'

'And how did that make you feel?'

'How do you think? Resentful. Angry. Yes, I was angry with him.'

'But surely you know your father had his own financial problems,' Llewellyn put in.

'No.' She turned a stony face to Llewellyn. 'Why should I have known? He rarely talked about the business. He knew we weren't really interested.'

'Maybe if you'd taken an interest he'd have lent you the money,' Llewellyn put in.

'Maybe. But it's academic now, isn't it?'

'Never mind,' said Rafferty. 'As I understand it, you're down for something from your father's life insurance policy.'

'Really?'

Was that 'really' a little disingenuous? Rafferty wondered. Could she and the rest of the family have been unaware of the terms of the policy? Keith Sutherland had reputedly been careless with his keys; any one of them could have taken the opportunity when they were left lying around and poked about his home office.

'Why did you particularly want to speak to your father alone? Didn't you want your mother to know you'd asked him for money?'

'No. She'd only worry. I preferred her not to know. I still do,' she added defensively. 'So I'd rather you didn't tell her.'

Rafferty nodded. 'It's all the same to me, Miss Sutherland. I won't tell her unless I find it necessary during the course of my investigations.'

She nodded acknowledgement. 'Thank you. And by the way, just so's you know, I didn't kill my father in a fit of pique. I didn't kill him at all.'

And with that, for now, they had to be satisfied.

Rafferty was in the police canteen having some lunch when Tom Kendall plonked his tray on the table and sat opposite. He didn't like the satisfied expression Tom wore. He liked the explanation for it even less.

'Seeing as you were so interested in my electrical warehouse case, I thought you'd like to know I've made some progress,' he said.

'Oh yes?' Rafferty tried to act nonchalant. 'What's happened?'

'Some of the stolen goods have turned up. Paul Perkins had another lock-up. We got a tip off. He's in the cells waiting for his brief to arrive. I'd like to see him wriggle out of this one now.'

Rafferty chewed his meat and potato pie, then asked, 'Has he said anything?'

'Not yet. He demanded a brief as soon as he was brought in. I doubt he'll say anything, but I reckon we've got him bang to rights. It's his lock-up, in his name and he has the only key – he admitted that much. If he gives me details of the customers who bought the stolen goods off him I might promise to see if I can't get him a reduced sentence. He knows the score. I reckon he'll cough sooner or later for a lesser term.'

211

Rafferty had lost his appetite. He left the rest of his meal although he'd only taken half a dozen mouthfuls. The part of the pie he *had* eaten sat heavily in his gut and threatened to give him indigestion for the rest of the afternoon.

Tom asked him if he wanted his pie and Rafferty shook his head.

'What's up, Joe? Case going badly?' Tom asked as he helped himself to Rafferty's pie.

'Something like that.' *One* case, anyway, he thought, horrified at Kendall's revelations. His ma would have to get rid of her latest purchase now, he reasoned. Even she must see that. Mustn't she?

Rafferty spent the rest of the day on tenter-hooks, waiting for Tom Kendall to come in and point the finger. It meant he got little work done. It also meant that his lack of productivity piqued Llewellyn's curiosity.

'What's the matter?' he eventually asked, after Rafferty had shifted restlessly in his chair and taken several hours to read one statement, none of which he had retained.

'There's nothing the matter,' Rafferty replied brusquely. 'I've got guts ache, that's all.'

'Have you taken something for it?'

'Who are you? My mother? And yes, I have taken something for it. It just hasn't

212

worked, that's all.'

Llewellyn rustled in his desk and came up with a packet of Rennies. He threw them over. 'Try them. They should do the trick.'

Rafferty gave a strained smile and swallowed the tablets down with cold dregs of tea. He wished all his problems could be so easily solved. However, after that and to assuage Llewellyn's further curiosity, he tried to settle down to reading the latest paperwork, while keeping his ears attuned to the noises from the corridor outside his door and for the sound of Tom Kendall's heavy tread. The fact that it didn't appear all afternoon didn't ease his anxiety one bit.

When Rafferty went round to his ma's home after work and told her the latest, she still denied she had anything to hide.

'You'll be done, Ma,' he warned her again. 'Tom Kendall, the DI in charge of the electrical warehouse jobs is confident that Paul will cough up the names of his customers. If you're one, the fact that I'm a copper won't save you. Do you want a criminal record?'

'It's yourself and your precious police career you're concerned about, Joseph, why don't you admit it?'

'Well yes, of course I'm concerned about that. Why wouldn't I be? It's my livelihood,

213

after all. But I'm concerned about you, too. Do you want your name in the local paper? Do you want her next door to know you've bought stolen goods? You'll never hear the end of it, you must know that. You know how keen she is to get one over on you.'

Ma's neighbour, 'Her Next Door', was in permanent competition with ma. Her nose had been seriously put out of joint when ma had become a great-grandmother first, albeit the child had been born to Gemma, his unmarried niece, with a boyfriend who had taken to his heels when the prospect of fatherhood beckoned.

If his concerns about his mother getting a criminal record hadn't bothered his ma, the prospect of her neighbour crowing about it seemed to have the desired effect.

For the first time, his ma admitted that she might, just possibly, have bought dodgy gear.

'Where is it?' Rafferty asked.

'Upstairs, in the spare bedroom.'

'We'll have to move it. It *is* a telly, I take it?'

'Yes. I bought it for your wedding.' Her lips pursed. 'I thought you'd be pleased. It's a plasma set, whatever that is. I remembered you mentioning you wanted one, so when the chance came my way I snatched it. I thought you'd be pleased,' she repeated

214

crossly. 'It's the last time I buy you anything,' she told him.

Rafferty was relieved to hear it. If only he could believe it. He'd have to wait till later, when it was dark, to shift the telly. He'd also have to get Mickey to give him a hand. The next question was where to stash it. After getting Mickey out from under in their last murder investigation, his brother owed him a favour. Besides, he didn't think Mickey would object to giving houseroom to a brand new plasma telly.

'Up your end. Careful. You nearly dropped it,' Rafferty warned.

'No I didn't,' Mickey contradicted. 'Come on. Let's get on with it before your colleagues raid the place.'

'Don't say that, for God's sake,' Rafferty protested. 'You're talking about my worst nightmare. Let's just get it shifted to your place and I'll be happy.'

Mickey grinned. 'Not nearly as happy as me. I've wanted a plasma TV for ages. More fool you for turning your nose up.'

'I'm a copper, Mickey, remember? It's more than my job's worth to be caught in possession of stolen goods. Come on. Down the stairs. Adjust that blanket. We don't want the neighbours to see what we're shifting.'

Mickey pulled the blanket more closely over the box and began to back down the stairs.

Finally, after negotiating the bend in the stairs, they made it up the garden path and stashed the box in Mickey's van. At last, Rafferty began to relax. He couldn't believe it when ma's next-door neighbour came out of her front door and followed them up the path.

'Is that the plasma telly your ma got you for your wedding?' she asked Rafferty.

Rafferty stared at her, unsure what to say. Should he confirm or deny it? He stood there frozen by indecision. It was left to Mickey to cheerfully confirm what the neighbour had said.

Briefly, Rafferty closed his eyes and wished for the ground to swallow him up. The damn telly was supposed to be a *secret*, God dammit, he thought. Why did both his ma and Mickey have to blab about it to the biggest gossip in the street? His ma had doubtless been boasting in their never-ending one-upmanship war. Surely, given that the wretched television had been half-inched, she could have been a bit more discreet, if only for his sake.

But it was too late now. All he could do was to get the damn thing shifted to Mickey's place and hope the heat died down.

Rafferty decided it would be a good idea to question Ian Sutherland's friends again. By now they might have thought again about the advisability of lying to the police – if indeed they had done so.

He had Llewellyn ring Gavin Harold and Chris Tennant to make an appointment. He'd try to see Rick Wentworth and Sanjay Gupta on Sunday.

Gavin Harold turned out to be in a garrulous, ebullient mood; as he explained, he'd just pulled off a coup to sell software to a major national company. He was cock-a-hoop and it may have made him keep less of a guard on his tongue than might otherwise be the case. So when Rafferty introduced the topic of Ian Sutherland's finances, Harold let slip that it wasn't only the costs of his wedding and the go-slow in his business finances that weighed heavily on Ian's shoulders.

'Poor old Ian, he'd got several other large debts and spends half his time dodging the collectors. I've had him camped out on my sofa many times recently, too scared to go home.'

'Yes, I'd heard he was deeply in hock,' Rafferty lied. 'He must be relieved he'll soon get his inheritance.'

'Lord, yes. He told me he's down for a fair pile from the life insurance. Looks like daddy came up trumps for once. It'll get him out of a lot of trouble.'

'I wondered if you'd had any more thoughts about the night of Keith Sutherland's murder. You said when we first questioned you that Ian had been with you all the time once you'd left The Railway Arms. Perhaps now you've had time to think you'd like to alter your statement?'

Gavin Harold's eyes narrowed. 'No. I don't think so. That's pretty much as I remember it.'

'But is your memory that clear? You'd been drinking most of the evening and into the early hours, after all.'

Harold shrugged. 'It's as clear as I can remember and that is that Ian was with us the entire time. There's nothing else I can add.'

That being that and nothing else to be gained, they left soon after.

'Maybe Chris Tennant will be more forthcoming,' said Rafferty as they got in the car.

'It's interesting to learn that Ian Sutherland has other debts than just the wedding expenses. It gives him another reason to want his father dead and it's clear he knew about the life insurance. I can't believe he didn't mention it to his mother and sister.'

218

'Nor can I,' said Rafferty as Llewellyn turned the car towards Tennant's flat.

Chris Tennant wasn't quite as garrulous in his welcome as had been Gavin Harold. He let them in and gave a heavy sigh as he shut the door. 'What now?' he demanded. 'I'm beginning to wish I'd never gone to Ian's bloody stag do.'

He invited them to sit down and flung himself into an armchair. 'I've told you all I know. I don't know what else I can say.'

Rafferty asked him again about his recollections of the night of Sutherland's murder.

'To be honest, it's all a bit hazy now. The better the night, the hazier the memories is what I find. Sorry I can't be more helpful.'

And that was that. There was nothing to be gained by questioning Tennant further. A drunken lads' night out wasn't the best basis for extracting reliable evidence. They gave up for the day, returned to the station and went their separate ways.

The next day was another busy one. To Rafferty's surprise, the mystery man who had been in the snug of The Railway Arms turned up at the station voluntarily. He wanted to clear his name, he said. But it turned out he was only twenty minutes ahead of a neighbour who had recognized him from the photofit the landlord, Andy

219

Strong, had provided.

Hugo Davenport, for such was the mystery man's name, claimed he had dropped into The Railway Arms by chance, and had met Keith Sutherland also by chance.

'You're certain you didn't have an arrangement to meet Mr Sutherland?'

'No. No way. As I said, I was in the area and thought I'd drop in for a quick one, that's all. I was surprised to see Keith.' He paused, then added, hurriedly, as if he thought he ought to express some grief for his old friend, 'Of course I was shocked when I learned of his death. Tragic. Quite tragic.'

If Hugo Davenport truly thought Keith Sutherland's death a tragedy no grief showed in his eyes. In fact, an air of relief seemed to cloak the man.

Rafferty excused himself from the interview room and went to telephone Mary Sutherland to see what she could tell him about Davenport.

She remembered the name. 'I never met him but Keith told me about him. That's the man who owed Keith a lot of money. Keith was pressing him for payment.'

'Is that so?' Here was yet another motive for murder. 'Had they arranged to meet in The Railway Arms do you know?'

'That's what Keith said. He told me he

was going to say to this Hugo that he'd take him through the courts if he didn't pay up.'

'Thanks for the information, Mrs Sutherland,' said Rafferty. Talk your way out of that one, Hugo, old son, he thought.

Hugo Davenport soon caved in when confronted with the truth.

'Yes. All right. I owed Keith money. But he was easy about it.'

'That's not what his wife says. She told me that Keith intended to pursue you through the courts for the money.'

Davenport shifted uneasily on his chair. 'That was only his way. I was talking him round. He liked to play the hard man, but he was soft as butter inside.'

'You weren't talking him round very successfully, I shouldn't think, given that Keith Sutherland had money worries of his own. He needed the money you owed him. How much was it, by the way?'

There was a brief pause, then Davenport replied, 'Ten grand.'

Given the other's pause for thought, Rafferty guessed the figure was double that.

'You'll owe it to his estate now. The debt won't die with him.'

'It might. I doubt if his widow will pursue it with any tenacity.'

'Perhaps not. I doubt if the same can be

said of her lawyers.'

Davenport blanched at the mention of this nasty word and went quiet.

'We'll need your address, sir,' Rafferty told him. 'We need to know where to contact you as we are likely to want to speak to you again.'

Davenport, his expression abject, gave it.

The interviews later that afternoon with Rick Wentworth and Sanjay Gupta, the other members of the stag party, went much as expected. Like Gavin Harold and Chris Tennant, they claimed their memories were seriously impaired.

'Which,' as Rafferty told Llewellyn as they left the last of the pair, 'leaves Ian Sutherland with some serious deficiencies in his alibi. His friends mostly seem to be too busy reversing out of trouble to back him up now. And given that he was desperate for money...'

'It's still a very tight timeline for him to have committed the murder,' Llewellyn pointed out.

'Yet it takes less than a minute to kill someone. After all, he knew his father was thrown out of the pub at the same time as himself and his friends, knew he'd be fumbling around in the ill-lit car park, looking for his car and his keys. It would have been a matter of moments only to follow him into the car park and kill him.'

'But surely he wouldn't have brought a knife out with him on his stag night?'

'Why not? Lots of young men habitually carry knives. Maybe, as part of the stag-night entertainment, they intended to pick a fight with someone. To some people that would be the perfect way to end a good night out.'

Llewellyn gave a moue of distaste for such low elements of society, but he made no more objections to Rafferty's reasoning. 'So do you want to question Ian Sutherland again?' he asked now.

Rafferty shook his head. 'Not yet. Let him stew. He'll know soon enough from his friends that we've been questioning them again – though whether they'll admit they've been backtracking in their support for his alibi is another question.

'No,' he said decisively, 'you and me, Dafyd, are going to read and digest this little lot.' He slapped the top of the latest statements. 'There might be a gem in here somewhere.'

But after several fruitless hours reading, no such gem had appeared and Rafferty gave up in disgust and went home.

The next morning, he felt unaccountably

optimistic. He entered the office bright, breezy and full of goodwill to all men. He didn't even come down with a bump when Llewellyn told him the latest CCTV viewings had yielded nothing.

Llewellyn said, 'Jonathon Lilley has found out something interesting.'

Rafferty swung his chair back from his contemplation of the weather. 'Oh yes?'

Llewellyn nodded. 'Apparently Mrs Sutherland and Mr Derek Fowler were close some years ago. Before they were both married. Quite a serious relationship. Almost came to an engagement, but then they broke up.'

'You're thinking of the possibility of collusion, I take it?'

Llewellyn nodded again. 'Though, in fairness, I have to add that there's not a whisper of anything between them recently.'

'Even so, it brings up an interesting possibility. Maybe they plan to split the proceeds once SuperElect is sold to the buyout firm. It would mean getting rid of hubby would be a profitable pursuit. It might be worth getting Lilley to check round the pubs, restaurants and motels to see if anyone's seen Fowler and a woman matching Mary Sutherland's description together. You've got a copy of that photo of Derek Fowler?'

Llewellyn nodded.

'Let Lilley have it. It might turn up a new lead.'

Llewellyn nodded and went out.

When Rafferty got home that evening, he and Abra sat down and thrashed out their wedding arrangements.

They'd already agreed on the venues for the ceremony and reception and they'd paid a deposit on the honeymoon cottage. All that remained was the rest.

Rafferty quickly agreed to drop his choice of photographer; even he had to admit that a man who shot pictures of houses for a living wasn't ideal. He acknowledged it had been a daft idea. It was the desire to keep the costs down that had spurred him on and which had led to their three-month split. He wouldn't make that mistake again.

'Who did Llewellyn use at his and Mo's wedding?' he asked.

'They're no good. They were booked up when I rang them.'

'Try them anyway. There's many a slip between the proposal and the wedding.' As there had so nearly been between him and Abra. 'They may get a cancellation for the day. In fact, it might be an idea to put in for cancellations with all your preferred photographers. We're bound to get lucky with one of them.'

Llewellyn's mother-in-law was to make the wedding cake – three tiers rather than the five Abra had originally wanted. And Llewellyn had already designed and printed off the invitations. 'What about the caterers?'

'I don't think we're going to get them any cheaper,' Abra told him. 'We're just going to have to grin and bear the cost.'

Rafferty nodded. 'What about the bridesmaids? We'll need to get them gifts.'

'Don't worry. I've got that in hand. And as for Dafyd, I thought a pair of cufflinks. You know what a snappy dresser he is.'

Dafyd was to be his best man.

'What about these favours for the guests that Dafyd mentioned? Are they absolutely essential?'

Abra shook her head. 'No. They're a nice touch, but they're just a way to extract more money. We can do without them.'

'And what about the guest list? Can we cut it down a bit?'

The guest list ran to two hundred and was still growing. Rafferty didn't think he *knew* two hundred people, certainly not most of this lot.

Abra pulled a face. 'I've already asked most of them,' she admitted.

Dismayed, Rafferty picked up his glass

and took a swig of Jameson's. 'OK,' he said. 'Let's go through the list and put a cross against the names of those you *haven't* asked.'

'We can't put a cross against all of them. Some of them are people to whose weddings we've been to. We've got to reciprocate.'

Rafferty didn't see why, but he didn't argue, just went through the guest list with Abra and got her to at least cross *some* of the names off.

That done, he sat back with a relieved sigh. They'd got through it without a row, which was a big improvement on their previous efforts.

Another drink was called for. Rafferty poured them out while Abra tidied the wedding lists back into the white box file she'd bought specially.

When she'd finished tidying things away, Rafferty raised his glass. 'Cheers. Here's to us.'

'To us.' They chinked glasses.

Abra grinned. 'Funny to think the wedding's back on. When you consider what we might have been doing instead. What do you think you might have been doing tonight?'

Leading a sad-git existence, thought Rafferty. Me and my dinners for one. 'Out with Mickey, probably,' he lied. Truth was, he'd never gone out with his little brother that much. Mickey had his own friends and generally preferred to keep Rafferty on the periphery of such friendships. 'How about you?'

'Oh, deciding which of my large circle of admirers to go out with.'

Rafferty's face fell. 'Oh.' His gaze narrowed. 'Was there anyone serious?'

Abra laughed. 'No. Don't worry, Joe. I'm only teasing. Like you, I'd probably have stayed in and washed my hair. Just as well we're marrying each other as no one else seems to want either of us.'

'The more fool them. We're a fine pair of catches. Certainly *you* are.'

'Thank you, kind sir. You're not so bad yourself. Seriously though – did you meet anyone else during the weeks we were apart?'

Rafferty shook his head. 'No. I wasn't looking. I was waiting for you to come to your senses and realize what a fine specimen of manhood you were letting slip through your fingers.'

Abra threw a cushion at him. 'Smug git.'

'But you did, though, didn't you? Come to your senses, I mean?' Rafferty asked with a wry smile.

It was a smile Abra was quick to match. 'Yes. I suppose I did. Are you glad?'

'Too right. I'm very glad.'

'Me too.' She snuggled into his arms while the soft music he had put on the stereo serenaded them.

FIFTEEN

'You seem pretty sure that Andy Strong didn't kill Sutherland. So what about Sutherland's son?' Bradley demanded. 'The MOMs seem to be stacked against him.' The means, opportunity and motive.

'Motive and opportunity, anyway. As to the means, we have no proof that Ian Sutherland was carrying a knife. And we have failed to find one on his route from the pub to the club.'

'He had motive and opportunity, that's enough for me. He'll have got rid of the knife. He's favourite for me,' Bradley insisted. 'He should be favourite for you, too.'

Well, he was and he wasn't. Yes, Bradley was right – the MOMs were stacked up against Ian Sutherland. But that didn't mean he'd killed his father. But if he hadn't – who had? Round and round went Rafferty's mind while Superintendent Bradley

229

harangued him.

'I want some results on these murders, Rafferty, and I want them soon. See to it.'

Rafferty nodded. It wasn't an acquiescent nod, more of an expedient one and an acknowledgement of Bradley's diatribe. But he still felt it committed him to something.

Ho hum. What to do? Ian Sutherland was in the frame, there was no doubt about that. He might not have all three of the MOMs, but he had two out of three.

Where was the knife? That was the question. They hadn't found it. They'd searched thoroughly, but there was no sign of it. Part of him wanted to do what Bradley asked – demanded – and arrest Ian Sutherland. But another part of him wasn't sure of Sutherland's guilt. But where else was he to go? Who else could he arrest? As Bradley had said, Ian Sutherland had the motive and opportunity. Had he carried the means also? And if so, what had he done with it?

Rafferty was tired of thinking about it. He was tired of Bradley pushing him. He needed to do something.

The investigation into Carol Mumford's murder was progressing about as satisfactorily as the one into Keith Sutherland's. Apart – obviously – from the person who killed her, she had no known enemies. And given the fact and method of her murder, it seemed that even Carol Mumford herself hadn't known the person was an enemy.

Rafferty had divided the investigation team in two. He had learned as much about the two victims as an investigating officer would possibly want to know, but it seemed to have gained him little. He was no nearer to solving either crime now than he had been at the beginning.

Llewellyn was as stumped as he was, which was unusual. The Welshman usually managed a few kernels of insight during investigations. The fact that he had mentioned few at least made Rafferty feel less lacking in investigatory skills than he otherwise might have.

They'd checked with Carol Mumford's work colleagues, friends and family as carefully as they'd checked those of Keith Sutherland, but had little to show for all the effort expended. Both cases seemed to have shunted themselves into sidings. And it was up to him to bring them back on track. And of course, he had Superintendent Bradley on his case. He'd been the same ever since he'd caught him inspecting the inside of his eyelids. Bradley had made clear he thought he was falling asleep on the job and needed regular prodding if he was to get anywhere.

Who stood to gain was the question. And

it was easily answered: on the one hand, the dead man's family and on the other, Derek Fowler and his wife.

But Derek Fowler had been in Cambridge and no amount of questions had been able to place him in Elmhurst on the night of Sutherland's murder. And for all she had been on the spot, try as he might, Rafferty couldn't see the twittery Mrs Fowler managing to stick a knife between someone's shoulder blades.

So that left the family ... Mary, Susie and Ian Sutherland. The picture was narrowing and it now seemed more likely that one of the three were guilty. Of the three, it seemed more likely that it had been Ian. Knifing was generally a male crime. The sheer physicality of it met some need in the male psyche that didn't exist in that of the female, or not nearly as often.

But although they could find no evidence that Derek Fowler had been in Elmhurst on the night of the murder, it would be unwise to strike his name from the list of suspects. They'd circulated the local train stations and taxi firms with his description in case he'd left his easily identifiable car in Cambridge and used other means of travel. But it wasn't as if he had any physical peculiarity to mark him out from the hordes of other middle-aged, paunchy males. Certainly, no one had claimed to have seen him. Of course, if he'd been intent on murder, Fowler might have disguised himself in some way. There was just no telling.

Tom Kendall popped his head round Rafferty's office door. 'Thought you'd like to know,' he said, 'that Paul Perkins is singing louder than Placido Domingo. And although he has yet failed to implicate his two brothers, he's stitched up the two lads who worked in the last two warehouses that were done and has started to squeal about the customers who bought the hookey gear.'

'He has?' Dismayed, Rafferty could think of nothing to say beyond, 'Come up with many names, has he?'

'Ten so far and counting.'

'Anyone we know?'

'No one *I* know. Maybe you'll be familiar with a few of the names.' Quickly Tom consulted a list which he pulled from his pocket and rattled the names off. Thankfully, ma's wasn't amongst them. Yet. But Tom had said that Paul Perkins was still spilling beans. It was possible he'd spill ma's name before the day was out. He was only thankful that he'd at least persuaded her that it would be a good idea to move the telly.

Rafferty felt sick. It was as much as he could do to congratulate Kendall on his success. Though he wasn't sure he'd made a convincing job of it.

They'd yet to talk to Ian Sutherland about what he'd been doing in the gents' toilet of The Railway Arms around eleven on the night of his father's murder, when he'd denied going in there at that time. They had also yet to question Mary Sutherland about her previous close relationship with Derek Fowler. They might both be significant and it was important to get answers to both questions.

They set off after Rafferty had had a rejuvenating cup of hot, sweet tea.

They went to see Ian Sutherland first, at his place of work. They hadn't bothered to make an appointment and they had to wait in the outer office as he was with clients when they got there.

Rafferty took the time to look around; the agency wasn't nearly as swish as his cousin Nigel's, which was all chrome and leather. The decoration and furniture in the outer office looked a little tired, much like Sutherland himself, whom they could see through the glass dividing his office from the main room, sitting behind his desk with a desperate look on his face. Rafferty guessed his persuasion of the couple with him to buy or sell wasn't going well.

There were six desks in the outer office, but only two of them were occupied. The other desks were clear and indicated that the staff who had used them had been let go. Even the property details displayed in the windows and on the walls were limited and looked a little dog-eared as if they had been pinned up for some time. It seemed that Nigel had been right in his supposition of how Sutherland's business was going.

The two members of staff on duty didn't seem to have much to do: one seemed to be covertly perusing the situations vacant columns in the local paper and the other was staring out the window watching the rain obliterate the few property details behind the glass.

The couple in with Sutherland were only there for another five minutes and didn't look very happy when they came out of his office. Rafferty heard them muttering about shifting their property to another agency as it wasn't moving. He walked across to the open office door and knocked.

'Mr Sutherland.' His office looked in a better state of repair than the outer office, but it still presented a less than pristine and successful appearance. Rafferty wondered how much longer he could keep going.

Sutherland looked harassed and haggard, worse than when he'd been nursing a hangover after his stag party.

'Oh no,' he said. 'Not again. How much longer is this going to go on?'

'Until we find your father's murderer, sir,' Rafferty told him. 'Tell me something, Mr Sutherland, about the night of your father's murder.'

'Tell you what? I've told you all I know.'

'No you haven't. Not quite. For instance, you told me that you didn't visit the lavatory just before you left the pub, yet I have a witness who places you there just before eleven that night. Why did you lie to me?'

Sutherland looked shaken. 'I ... I must have forgotten, that's all. It was a heavy night. I told you that.'

'Yes. But it's strange that none of your friends recalled the visit to the gents', either. They all at first claimed you were together the entire time before they started claiming alcoholic amnesia.' Was the visit to the gents' an excuse so he could lag behind and slip round to the car park and murder his father before he caught his friends up?

'I can't help their memories. I'm only responsible for my own. And I told you I simply forgot. Does it matter?'

'It might, Mr Sutherland, if you were deliberately delaying leaving in order to follow your father round to the car park.'

Sutherland looked shocked at this suggestion. 'You can't seriously think that I'd kill the old man? Sure, we had our differences, but it's not as if we saw that much of each other that we couldn't live with them.'

In view of Sutherland's vehement denials, Rafferty decided to try another tack. 'Business seems to be quiet today. And I see you've let some of your staff go. Things not going well?'

'It's just a temporary blip. Once business picks up I'll take on some more people.'

'How long's it been this quiet?'

'Not long. A few months, that's all. Every firm in this business has been feeling the pinch a little with the credit crunch, we're not the only ones.'

No, but it confirmed Sutherland's urgent need for money. And given that he had been on the spot when his father died, things weren't looking good for him.

Having achieved his object, as well as seriously rattling the man, Rafferty led Llewellyn out and back to the car.

From Sutherland's, they drove to see his mother. Mary Sutherland was again alone; perhaps Susie had gone in pursuit of another bank loan for her business. There was no Family Liaison Officer with her – she had said she preferred to be alone with her daughter and the officer had been withdrawn. Rafferty would have preferred for the police presence in the house to continue, it being possible that, if either woman had anything to conceal, they might let something slip.

She offered them tea or coffee and Rafferty accepted; he wanted to get his thoughts in order and decide how best to bring up the subject of Derek Fowler. However, the tea-making didn't take long and she was soon back, bearing a tray, which the ever-gentlemanly Llewellyn took from her and placed on the coffee table.

'What did you want to talk to me about, Inspector?' she asked as she poured the tea. 'Are you any nearer to finding out who killed my husband?'

'As to that, we're making progress and eliminating certain possibilities. We're hopeful that the eliminations will lead us to the killer. But what I wanted to speak to you about was your relationship with Derek Fowler.'

'My relationship with—' She broke off. 'There is no relationship. We rarely socialized.'

'Not now, maybe. But it's my understanding that at one time, before either of you married, you and Mr Fowler were close. I heard you were practically engaged.'

She laughed. 'My God, that's ancient history. And to put the record straight, we weren't "practically engaged". We never came close to that. It was just the usual boy and girl romance that petered out as these things do.'

'I see. You didn't find it difficult that he was in partnership with your husband?'

'No. Not at all. I told you, I rarely saw him. Our relationship as you call it was in the past. A very long time in the past.' She sipped her tea. Rafferty noticed that, in spite of her calm appearance, her hand was shaking slightly. 'Is that all you wanted to see me about?'

'Yes. That's all.' He finished his tea and stood up. 'Sorry to have bothered you.'

'It was no bother, Inspector. You must bother me as much as you like until you find my husband's killer.'

She showed them out.

'We don't seem to be progressing much, do we?' Rafferty asked Llewellyn. 'Mary Sutherland certainly didn't seem at all disconcerted that we had discovered her previous relationship with Fowler.' Though there had been that slight trembling of the hand holding her cup. Could be significant.

'No. Makes one think that what she claimed is true and there is no current relationship, which would seem to indicate that there is no collusion between them.'

'As you say, no collusion between those

239

two. It doesn't mean that there couldn't have been collusion between her and her son and daughter. Both were in the vicinity of The Railway Arms on the night of Keith Sutherland's death. All have reasons to want him dead. And all we have to do is prove it. Come on, let's get back.' Rafferty was keen to return to the station and find out if Paul Perkins had blabbed any more names.

The rain had stopped while they were speaking to Mary Sutherland. It had left large puddles on the pavement and they walked a meandering path to the car to avoid them.

Rafferty was filled with anxiety as they came through from the back entrance to reception, wondering if news of his ma's misdeed had been found out and was already whizzing its way round the station.

But everything was quiet. Bill Beard, usually the first to hear any gossip, greeted him normally with no hint of secrets discovered about him. But the waiting was getting to him. Part of him was beginning to wish ma would be found out; at least he wouldn't feel he had to creep around like a criminal once it was discovered. But of course the reality of discovery would be infinitely worse than the anticipation – Superintendent Bradley would make sure of that.

Rafferty climbed the stairs to his second-floor office, followed by Llewellyn. He checked his in-tray, but nothing new had come in. He felt at a loss as to where to go on the case. He had nothing firm, nothing conclusive on any of the suspects, apart, perhaps from Ian Sutherland. He'd questioned the main ones several times, but had drawn nothing useful from any of them. He desperately needed something to break.

SIXTEEN

There was nobody more surprised than Rafferty when something did break. It had been quiet all afternoon. The phone had barely rung and even Paul Perkins's flow of information seemed to have dried up, without him, so far, having mentioned ma's name. The last thing he expected was for Bill Beard to ring up from reception to tell him that Mary Sutherland was downstairs and wanted to see him.

'I'll come down,' he said. Curious as to what she wanted, he took the stairs two at a time and hurried through the double doors to reception.

Mary Sutherland was seated on one of the benches lining the wall. She appeared anxious. Her greying hair looked as if she had been running nervous fingers through it. Her face was tense and tight-lipped. Rafferty guessed that she must have heard from Ian that he was pursuing her son as the main suspect. Had she come to protest his innocence?

'Mrs Sutherland. How can I help you?' he asked.

She stood up and clutched her handbag tightly. 'I wanted to talk to you about my son. About Ian.'

'Do you want to come up to my office?'

She nodded and followed him through the doors and up the stairs.

Once he had her settled in one of the visitor's chairs, she burst out: 'Ian didn't kill his father. You've got to know that. He's not capable of such a violent act. I know he isn't.'

'You may, Mrs Sutherland,' he told her, ' but I don't. There's a lot of circumstantial evidence pointing to him.'

'Are you ... are you going to arrest him?' She sat forward edgily on her chair and stared at him from fear-filled eyes.

'As to that, we'll have to see,' he said. 'I've a few more aspects of the case I need to investigate.' He wished he knew what they were. 'But I may well be inviting your son into the station for a more formal interview shortly as his memory seems shaky in several areas.'

'But he was drunk. It's natural that he can't remember certain things. It was his stag night, for God's sake. Of course he had one over the eight. It's what young men do on their stag nights. I don't think it's fair that you're holding it against him.' She sat forward on her chair, her entire body seemed clenched in anxiety as she stared at him, desperate to convince him of her own belief in her son's innocence.

'His friends' memories also seem shaky,' Rafferty told her. 'In fact they've started to backtrack on what they originally told me.' He didn't know why he was telling her all this. He supposed it was because she looked so desolate, so desperate, clutching her handbag to her like a shield. He wondered what she had thought she would achieve by coming to him like this and protesting her son's innocence. If it was doing anything, it was making him more, not less, convinced of Ian's guilt. Had Ian put her up to it? Or was it entirely her own idea?

She must have read his mind, for she said, 'Ian doesn't know I'm here. He'd probably tell me I was wasting my time.'

So would Rafferty; in fact, he had, in so

many words.

She seemed to realize it, for she clutched her bag even more determinedly and stood up. 'I can see my coming here has made it worse for Ian rather than better. I won't take up any more of your time.'

Rafferty gestured to Llewellyn at the corner desk, who had been taking notes of the conversation, to escort her back downstairs. He was back in five minutes.

'Wonder what brought that on,' he said.

'I think it must have got back to her that we have been showing quite an interest in young Ian,' said Rafferty. 'I wonder what she hoped to achieve by coming here?'

'Perhaps she was just on a fishing expedition. She certainly found out your intentions. Why were you so forthcoming?'

'God knows. Let's hope Ian Sutherland doesn't do a runner. After all, with his business apparently about to go under, he has little to lose. Maybe we ought to get round to his place now and make good my threat of arrest?'

'Don't you think you're being a little precipitate? Everything we have is just circumstantial.'

Rafferty put on his jacket. 'Circumstantial or not, there's enough there to justify an arrest. Coming?' He still wasn't entirely convinced of Sutherland's guilt, but maybe, in custody and with what he said down on tape, Sutherland's memory would improve.

Ian Sutherland seemed subdued when they rang his bell and came quietly. He didn't even protest his innocence more than once. He said little beyond what he'd already said once they got him into an interview room.

'You don't deny that you knew about the money you would receive from your father's life insurance policy?'

'No. I knew about it. And yes, I needed the money. You saw how my business is fixed. But I didn't kill him for what I'd get out of him. I'm not guilty and you can't prove I did it.'

'People have been convicted on less circumstantial evidence than what we've got on you,' Rafferty told him. 'You were on the spot. We've evidence that you loitered in the gents' toilets, which you denied, and we've got the fact that you and your father didn't get on.' He pointed to the now fading bruise on Sutherland's chin. 'That tells us as much. So does the evidence of the landlord of The Railway Arms and the other customers.'

Ian Sutherland opened his mouth to protest, then clearly thought better of it. 'I want a solicitor,' he said instead.

'Of course. That's your prerogative. Do

you have a solicitor of your own or do you want the duty brief?'

'I'll have to make do with the duty brief. As you pointed out, my finances are poor. They won't stretch to my own solicitor.'

Rafferty formally cautioned him then and ended the interview. He sent Llewellyn off to contact the duty solicitor and instructed the uniformed officer outside the door to take Sutherland to a cell.

As soon as he'd disappeared through the door, Rafferty began to have doubts. Had he done the right thing? Had he acted too soon? Had he arrested the right person?

Now that he'd acted, he was reluctant to discuss his decision with Llewellyn: such a discussion was only likely to increase his doubts not lessen them. But he'd done it now. He'd have to tell Superintendent Bradley what he'd done. He doubted that Bradley would have any doubts. He'd been pushing for this arrest for some time – when he wasn't pressing him to arrest Andy Strong.

He took himself upstairs to his office. He then organized a search warrant for officers to go round to Sutherland's flat and look for the murder weapon. That done, he sat back and worried some more.

Uniformed found various knives in Ian

Sutherland's flat. They were all bagged up and sent to forensic. Now he'd have to wait and hope that one of them proved to be the murder weapon.

Ian Sutherland was formally interviewed with his solicitor present, but he volunteered little more beyond protesting his in-nocence once again, causing Rafferty's doubts to grow stronger. He put them to one side and concentrated on preparing the case for the Crown Prosecution Service.

Rafferty still had doubts about what he'd done the next morning, but he ploughed on with the paperwork. The facts all pointed to Ian Sutherland's guilt.

Two days later and Rafferty's doubts about Ian Sutherland's guilt had only increased. The man's demeanour was all wrong some-how, for a patricide. And then there was the knife. How would he have concealed a knife with an eight-inch blade in his stag night suit? The handle would have roughly doubl-ed the length of the weapon – surely it would have fallen out of an inside pocket at some point during that drunken stag night? The route Ian and his friends had taken from the pub to the Scorpio Club had been thoroughly searched as had the pub and the club. No knife had been found. There wasn't a trace of it and he didn't believe Ian

Sutherland would be so stupid as to put the murder weapon back in the rack in the kitchen with his other knives.

Yes, Rafferty was convinced he'd made a horrible mistake in arresting and charging Sutherland. But what to do about it now? Bradley would blow a gasket if he went to him and explained his doubts; he'd been cock-a-hoop about the arrest. Sutherland had been remanded in custody and had already entered the system.

As Bradley would tell him, Sutherland had been on the spot when his father died and had no alibi for the night of Carol Mumford's murder. The desperately needed inheritance was a powerful motivating factor for Ian Sutherland to kill his father and maybe, in Mumford's case, revenge for his mother's humiliation was motive enough. Even the desire to prevent Mumford from profiting from the £15,000 she'd been left by his father was another reason to kill her. And after the first murder, the second one would come so much more easily.

No, he'd get no help from Bradley. He'd have to carry on with the investigation on the sly then, between the other cases that had come in and landed on his desk.

He'd have to let Llewellyn in on what he intended; there was no way he could keep disappearing without the Welshman asking questions.

He glanced at Llewellyn as he sat hard at work on another case. 'Dafyd,' he asked, 'do you think I've made a terrible mistake on the Sutherland murder in arresting Ian Sutherland?'

Llewellyn stopped what he had been doing and turned round to face Rafferty. 'I think you might have been a bit precipitate,' he remarked. 'I said so at the time, if you recall.'

He had, too. Why hadn't he listened to him? Llewellyn invariably gave good advice, logical and to the point, even if, at times, it tended to verbosity.

'I want to carry on with the investigation,' Rafferty said now. 'And I'll need you to cover for me.' He was a bit dubious about Llewellyn's ability to lie for him; duplicity had never been the Welshman's strength. But there was no one else he could rely on.

'Have you suspicions of someone other than Sutherland?' Llewellyn asked.

'Well, I must have, mustn't I? But it's nothing concrete, just an uneasy feeling in my gut.' It had been there since he'd charged Ian Sutherland. He suspected that the only thing that would take it away was if he was to arrest the real murderer.

To Rafferty's surprise, Paul Perkins hadn't yet named ma as one of his customers. He didn't know why unless it was out of loyalty to an old market colleague. But he was very thankful for it. It meant he had one less thing to worry about as it didn't seem likely that at this late stage Perkins would add to his story.

Rafferty went home that night with his mind still wrestling with the Sutherland case. But he forced thoughts of it from his mind as he opened the door to the flat. After his and Abra's three-month relationship glitch, he was determined to do nothing that would jeopardize it. Not again. So he plastered a cheerful smile on his face as he opened the living-room door and held up the bag containing the takeaway that he'd picked up on the way home.

'I got us an Indian,' he told her as he made for the kitchen.

'Great. I hadn't even started to think about dinner yet. What did you get?'

'What do you think? Your favourite, of course. Chicken Tikka Masala and plain rice.'

Abra invariably chose the same meal when they had an Indian. She was strangely unadventurous in her eating habits, whereas Rafferty liked to ring the changes. She always said she knew what she was getting with the chicken dish and that it held no unpleasant surprises for her.

'Shall I open some wine?' she asked now.

'Yeah. Open that expensive bottle that I bought last week.'

'It'll be wasted with spicy food. I'll open one of the cheapo ones instead. Let's save the other one for a special occasion, like when you solve your latest murders to your satisfaction.'

Rafferty had told Abra about his doubts over the case; he tried to share some of the details of his work with her, aware of how many wives and girlfriends became disenchanted with their partner's job. After so nearly losing her because of his intransigence over their wedding arrangements, he did his best to make sure his work didn't come between them.

He dished up the food and put some light music on the stereo to accompany the meal.

As she ate, Abra questioned him about the case. 'Have you told Bradley about your doubts?'

'You're joking.' Rafferty broke a poppadom and crunched his way through half of it. 'You know what he's like. He's only ever interested in results. And with Ian Sutherland under lock and key, he's got one – a double murder pretty speedily solved and that makes him look good. You'll have seen him on the local news preening and taking all the kudos. How do you think he'd react

251

if I went to see him and told him I felt I'd made a mistake?'

'Mmm. I see your problem. So what are you going to do?'

'The only thing I can do – carry on with the investigation, only on the quiet.'

'That's going to be difficult.'

'You can say that again. But I don't see what else I can do. Dafyd's agreed to cover for me on the occasions I go missing.'

'Dafyd?' Abra laughed. 'The man who, like George Washington, cannot tell a lie? That'll be a big help.'

Rafferty finished his meal and sat back, replete. 'He's the only cover I've got so I'll just have to hope for the best.' He wished he didn't feel that with his mother seemingly getting off scot free for her illegal purchase, he had already used up all his luck.

Rafferty began his covert investigation the following morning. First, he wanted to question Ian Sutherland's mother and sister. He was interested in their views about Ian's guilt or innocence.

He primed Llewellyn with a story about him going to speak to one of his snouts should Superintendent Bradley question him concerning his whereabouts.

Susie and Mary Sutherland were both at the family home when Rafferty called

252

round. Susie had been working on her laptop, which she went back to after she had let him in. Clearly, she didn't think he had anything of interest to say to them. Mary Sutherland was sitting plucking at her skirt and staring into space.

'I'm sorry to disturb you again, ladies,' he began. 'But I want to talk to you about Ian.'

'Haven't you disturbed us enough already?' Susie rounded on him. 'Wasn't charging Ian sufficient for you without trying to get us to incriminate him even further?'

'That's not my intention,' he told her. But it was clear she didn't believe him. Why should she, with her brother languishing in jail?

'Do you believe your son murdered his father?' he asked Mary Sutherland.

She stopped plucking at her skirt and raised her head. 'No, of course not. I know he didn't. It's just not in him to do such a thing. I've already told you that.'

For a moment, he thought she was going to say something more, but then she pursed her lips, subsided into silence and resumed plucking her skirt.

Susie ignored him until he came up behind her and closed the lid of her laptop. 'If you want to help your brother you should talk to me,' he told her.

'Why? Whatever we said you'd only twist it and use it against him. Why should we help you?' she challenged him again.

'Because I'm beginning to believe your brother didn't kill his father.' There – he'd said it. He waited for all hell to break loose at his confession, but both women only stared at him in amazement.

Eventually, Susie demanded, 'So why haven't you let him go?'

'It's not as simple as that. First I have to find the real killer – I need something substantial to justify releasing him and I haven't got it.'

'And you think we can help you? How?'

Rafferty shrugged. 'I don't know. I was hoping you could tell me.'

It was Susie's turn to shrug. 'I don't know what you possibly think we can tell you that will help. Ian was out with his friends on the night my father was killed and at home alone when that ... that woman was killed. We were neither of us anywhere near him, so how can we possibly help?'

Mary Sutherland opened her mouth. 'I—' she began, then stopped.

'Yes, Mrs Sutherland? You were going to say something?'

She stared at him then shook her head. 'Nothing. It was nothing.'

This was a waste of time, Rafferty acknowledged. Susie had been right. He shouldn't have come. But he had been convinced that either Ian's sister or mother knew something that could help him. His instincts were usually sound and it was disconcerting that they had led him astray this time.

He said his goodbyes and let himself out, wondering what he should do next to find the real killer, always assuming that his instincts about Ian Sutherland's innocence were correct. He didn't have a clue what to do next. The embarrassment factor involved in questioning the previous suspects was another difficulty. It felt ignominious to be in pursuit of someone else for the crime when he'd already made an arrest. It made him feel shabby and he didn't like that.

Rafferty went back to the station. Fortunately, Superintendent Bradley hadn't been on the prowl, hadn't interrogated Llewellyn as to his whereabouts. Like Abra, he doubted Llewellyn's ability to tell a convincing fib, so it was just as well. But such luck couldn't last. Perhaps it was just as well that he had no idea where he went from here.

Rafferty's conviction of Ian Sutherland's guilt had diminished with each hour that passed. Why had he been in such a tearing hurry to charge him? His reasons for this act seemed nebulous to him now. Not so to Superintendent Bradley, though. Bradley had seized on the arrest like a drowning man grasps and drowns a fellow swimmer. Nothing but clear-cut and indisputable evidence against another suspect would encourage him to leave go of this one.

Rafferty sighed. But who? How? Who else but Ian Sutherland had so many pointers to guilt? Of their other main suspects, Derek Fowler seemed a good choice. Due, on Keith Sutherland's death, to come in for the ownership of the entirety of SuperElect, he had a major motive for offing his partner.

The unfortunate thing was that they'd been unable to find any trace of him leaving Cambridge. Had they just not tried hard enough? How many ways *were* there to leave the university town? He could have taken his own, easily identified car; he could have hired a car – but all the car hire firms had been canvassed and came up blank. Ditto the railway staff at Cambridge, Elmhurst and all points in between. Private aircraft? That, too, had been looked into and dis-counted. They had even investigated the possibility of the journey having been made by river and sea and had still found no evidence of a stocky middle-aged man resembling Fowler taking ship. He was stumped. He didn't know where else to search for the elusive trace of the man.

And with no trace of Derek Fowler leaving Cambridge that left Doreen Fowler, who also stood to gain from Sutherland's death, courtesy of her husband's business agreement, and the two Sutherland women, Mary and Susie.

In his bones, he felt he could disregard Doreen Fowler. She just didn't seem to have the stuff of murder in her. And she seemed to have no more than a vague grasp of her husband's expectations on the business front.

Both of the Sutherland women also had financial expectations. Both seemed strong-enough characters to go in for murder. But had they?

Rafferty groaned. His head was spinning with the possibilities. He hunted through an overflowing desk drawer till he found some painkillers. He eased three out of the foil pack and swallowed them with the cold remnants of his tea.

He looked across at Llewellyn, who was industriously working his way through the latest statement dregs. 'Had any brain-waves?' he asked. 'Think it's possible Fowler burrowed his way here from Cambridge?'

Llewellyn smiled. 'I think we're going to have to discount Mr Fowler as a suspect. We have no sightings of him, nothing at all to indicate he left his Cambridge hotel.'

Rafferty gave a doleful nod. 'Such a shame. God knows he had motive enough to want Sutherland dead.'

'Yes, but with him, we're once again up against the question of why he would murder Carol Mumford. We seem to be able to find suspects in plenty for Keith Sutherland's killing, but only a few – namely the Sutherland family – with motive for killing Mumford.'

'Wish she wasn't included in the conundrum, our job would be a lot easier.'

'But she is and we have to find a killer with reason to murder both of them. Which brings us back to the Sutherlands.'

'Which brings us back to the Sutherlands,' Llewellyn agreed. 'The three of them are the only ones we've been able to pinpoint with motives for both murders. It seems to me we should concentrate rather more on them and less on the Derek Fowlers of this world.'

'That's what I was doing when I arrested Ian Sutherland,' Rafferty reminded him. 'And all that's done is make me full of doubts about my own certainties as to his guilt.'

'In that case, perhaps we should *cherchez la femme* – look for the woman, or women, in the case and investigate them a little more thoroughly.'

Rafferty nodded. 'We might as well. Because I'm damned if I know where else to go.'

And, at least, if nothing else, they were eliminating suspects.

SEVENTEEN

In spite of his uncertainty about what to do next, by the following morning Rafferty's subconscious had done his work for him. It was clear he had gone wrong somewhere in the investigation. So he would have to retrace his steps and go back over everything he had done. Hopefully, this time, it would lead him to the right person. More specifically and a lot more difficult, he would have to do it without Superintendent Bradley finding out. It was going to be a tall order.

He would start, as before, with Ian Sutherland's friends. Maybe their memories had improved by now.

He was lucky and found all four friends together in Gavin Harold's flat when he went to see Harold that evening.

Harold's expression hardened after he had opened the door and found Rafferty standing there.

'What do you want?' he demanded.

'Just a quiet word. I see your friends are here. That's handy. It will save me several journeys.'

'You want to come in?'

'That's the general idea.'

'What for? You've already got poor Ian in custody. Unless you're not satisfied with one victim and want to add to your tally.' It seemed that Gavin Harold had the hot temper of the true redhead. Rafferty didn't blame him for being angry on his friend's behalf; he'd have felt the same in his place.

'Nothing like that, Mr Harold. I've been having second thoughts about your friend's guilt and wondered if you and the rest of the stag party might have recalled something from that night that might help him.'

'It's a bit late for that, surely?'

'It's never too late, Mr Harold. Do you want to help your friend or not?'

'Yes, of course I do.' He stared reproachfully at Rafferty for several seconds, then said, 'You'd better come in.'

Gavin Harold's flat was a larger replica of Ian Sutherland's, with the same bare boards and leather settees. Also like Sutherland, the greater part of the fireplace wall was taken up with stereo, DVD player and a large TV screen with huge numbers of CDs and

DVDs stacked on shelves. His was a modern block rather than a converted terrace and had a pleasant river view. It must have cost him a packet. Rafferty hadn't realized just how much money there was in the computer game; shame he was so inept with the damn things or he too might have made his fortune.

Rafferty sat down beside Sanjay Gupta and told them what he'd told Gavin Harold. 'So you see, I need your help. My superintendent is convinced of Ian's guilt and wouldn't countenance us dropping the charges. Not unless I can come up with a suspect with something more than circumstantial evidence against them.'

'Circumstantial evidence was good enough for you to justify putting Ian away,' Gavin remarked.

'True.'

'Have you got anyone in mind?' Harold asked.

'Not yet. I'm hoping I'll be able to jog your memories of that night.'

'There's nothing to jog, man,' Harold told him. 'We told you all we knew the first time you questioned us. I don't see what else we can come up with. It's some time ago now.'

'I realize that. It's unfortunate. But there must be something else you remember. Some sound, perhaps, or a smell. Anything

261

at all that you noticed when you left the pub.'

The friends looked at one another, then Sanjay Gupta said, 'Funny you should mention a smell, because I did smell something that night. Some strong perfume. I remember thinking what a powerful pong it was.'

'That's good. That's the sort of thing I mean. Can you remember which way the wind was blowing that night? Was it coming towards you from the car park or from the road towards the car park?'

'It was coming from the car park. I remember 'cos it blew my hair over my face.'

Gupta sported hair to his shoulders.

'Did you smell the same scent in the pub?'

Gupta shook his head. 'I'd have noticed it for sure. It was overpowering.'

'Guppy's got a great sense of smell,' Chris Tennant told him. 'He wouldn't make a mistake like that. Besides, he hardly drank anything that night so I'm not surprised he's able to remember. He doesn't drink much at all. We drank his share.'

Rafferty nodded. He certainly hadn't noticed an overpowering perfume in the saloon bar and the only people in the snug had been Sutherland himself and Hugo Davenport. Which meant that whoever had worn it hadn't entered the pub, but *had* been in the car park, possibly for some time.

'That's very helpful,' he told them, as he felt the first glimmerings of excitement. 'Would you recognize the smell again?' he asked Sanjay.

'I might. I think so.'

Unfortunately, Rafferty hadn't noticed any of the suspects he had interviewed wearing a strong scent, neither the men nor the women. But it was something he hadn't known before. Why would someone who had been in the pub car park not go into the pub? There was nothing to keep anyone other than a car thief in the yard, unless the pongy-perfume wearer had been waiting for something. Or someone.

Rafferty cast his mind back to the scents he could recall during the case. Susie Sutherland had worn a light, barely there fragrance, not one that anyone could possibly call overpowering and her mother had worn no perfume at all. Derek Fowler, the late Keith Sutherland's business partner had worn a light, tangy aftershave. Rafferty had recognized it as it was one he also wore. As for the rest, either they had worn nothing, like Mary Sutherland, or the fragrance had faded to nothing by the time he had spoken to them. So unless he could check the contents of every suspect's bathroom he was no further forward.

Still, as he told himself again, it was something. 'Does anyone else remember anything significant?' he asked them.

'No,' said Gavin as the others shook their heads. 'I wish I could if it would help Ian. But there's nothing. Nothing at all.'

Rafferty stood up. 'Well, thanks for your time. You know where to find me if you remember anything else.'

Gavin Harold showed him out. 'And you know where to find *us* if you come up with anything.'

Rafferty nodded and headed for the lift. He drove home wondering if he should pay a visit to Boots' perfume department and check out the fragrances for strength. He could do worse. At least he'd be doing something.

The next morning found Rafferty waiting outside Boots for the store to open. As soon as it did, he hurried across to the perfume counter and attracted the attention of one of the assistants. 'I'm looking for a very strong perfume,' he told the girl when she came over.

She gave him an odd look and it struck Rafferty that she probably thought he was some sort of pervert.

'Did sir have anything particular in mind?'

'No. Just show me your strongest perfumes. It's a gift,' he improvised, 'for my great aunt who has a poor sense of smell.'

The girl smiled, clearly relieved that she wasn't dealing with an oddball after all.

'There's not much call for strong fragrances,' she told him. 'Most women prefer something subtle. But we have Vixen. That has a strong fragrance.' She named several other perfumes and brought them over for him to test.

'I'll take them all,' he said. 'How much is that?'

She named a figure that took his breath away even more than had the combined smell of his purchases. Next he went to the male fragrance counter and repeated the performance before taking his basket of perfumes to the pay desk. He only hoped this was going to achieve something other than an emptying of his wallet as it had just cost him a small fortune. But if Sanjay Gupta was able to identify the perfume he had smelt on the night of the murder he would be a step closer to the solution to the case. At least he hoped he would be.

He left the perfume in his car when he arrived at the station – he didn't want to invite speculation as to what he was doing buying a job lot of pongs.

He went upstairs to his office. Of course Llewellyn was there before him. Rafferty told him what he'd been doing that morning and why.

'And do you really think Sanjay Gupta will be able to remember and identify one particular smell after all this time?'

'That's what I'm hoping. I know it's a long shot. But it's worth a try.' But as Sanjay Gupta worked in London, he'd have to wait till this evening to test out his hopes. He'd have to bear his soul in patience till then. Of course it meant he'd be late home again, which wouldn't please Abra. He just hoped that when he explained his reasons for his late return she'd understand. If Gupta was able to pick out the particular perfume he'd smelt it might get them closer to a solution. It was the only clue he'd managed to come up with. But for now he had to knuckle down and get on with some of his official work. Currently, he had a vicious assault and a string of burglaries to get on with, so he settled down to studying what he had on them and did his best to put perfumes to the back of his mind.

Rafferty laid out the selection of perfumes and aftershaves on Sanjay Gupta's coffee table. 'Take your time,' he said. 'I don't want you to settle on one unless you're sure it's the perfume you smelt on the night of Mr Sutherland's murder.'

'OK. I'll do my best. Here goes.' One after another, Gupta picked up a perfume and sprayed it under his nose. By the time he tapped one of the perfumes and said, 'It was that one, I'm certain,' the room and Rafferty smelt like a tart's boudoir. He only hoped Abra believed him when he explained the reason for his exuberant fragrance...

He piled the perfumes back in their bag and thanked Sanjay. 'Sorry your living room had to end up with such a stink,' he said as Gupta threw open the windows.

'As long as it helps clear Ian, I don't care. I just hope identifying the perfume does the trick.'

So did Rafferty. He breathed in and started to gag. He immediately began to breathe through his mouth. The things he had to do in the cause of duty. Now all he needed to do was persuade various suspects to let him pay a visit to their bathrooms. It was going to be a bit tricky as they all knew that Ian Sutherland had been arrested for the killings as the report of his arrest had been on the TV and in the local paper, so it would be difficult enough persuading them to let him cross the threshold of their front doors, never mind being able to venture further. With Ian locked up for the double murder they'd wonder what he was doing visiting them at all.

EIGHTEEN

To Rafferty's surprise, gaining access to the suspects' bathrooms turned out to be surprisingly easy.

Derek Fowler, when Rafferty went to his home late the next morning, was at home and all genial bonhomie, doubtless brought about by his inheritance of Keith Sutherland's share of the business. His face was redder than ever and provided evidence that he'd had a celebratory drink or three, as did his whiskey breath.

'So, what can I do for you, Inspector? Tying up loose ends, is it?'

'Something like that, sir.'

Invited to sit down in the fussy, floral living room, he did so. 'I imagine you'll be planning your retirement now?'

'You imagine right. Keith could have been, too, if things had worked out differently. I awarded myself a day off today to get into the swing of retirement. Will you have a drink, Inspector? The sun must be approaching the yard arm somewhere in the world.'

'Not just now, thank you, sir. Tell me – what do you know of Ian Sutherland? For instance, did you know his business was on its uppers?'

Fowler nodded. 'His father said. He had a bit of a crow about it, as a matter of fact. Such a shame. If he'd only taken the offer from Electra he'd have been able to bail the boy out, perhaps see him through the credit crunch.'

'Would he have done so though, sir? You said he crowed about his son's difficulties.'

Fowler sighed. 'Perhaps you're right. Keith and his son didn't have a good relationship, something that was almost entirely Keith's fault. He didn't give Ian an easy time of it.'

'What about his daughter, Susie? What was his relationship with her like?'

'Better than it was with Ian, but still not easy. Basically, I don't think Keith was cut out to be a father. He was too selfish, for one thing.'

'What about his marriage? Was that relationship in a bad way, too? I've heard about his womanizing and know that Carol Mumford was his long-term mistress.'

'I think they just managed to rub along. Of course Keith didn't spend a lot of time at home. Between his women and his wheeling

269

and dealing, he was out a good deal.' He paused, then asked, 'Can I get my wife to get you a coffee, Inspector? Or tea, if you'd prefer.'

Rafferty hadn't seen Mrs Fowler since he'd arrived. 'No thank you.' He stood up. 'But could I use your bathroom? Too much tea at the station before I came out,' he explained.

'Of course. It's at the top of the stairs.'

Rafferty thanked him and made for the door. In the bathroom, he quickly checked the contents; there were no bottles of Vixen perfume. He came out to the top of the stairs and listened. There was no sound of movement from downstairs. He tiptoed along the landing and opened the first door. It contained a double bed and stuff on a dressing table, indicating that this was the marital room. He tiptoed again, treading carefully, anxious about creaking floorboards. No Vixen here, either. He crept his way back to the bathroom and pulled the chain of the toilet. Then he let the hot tap run for a few seconds. The pipes gurgled satisfactorily.

He thumped down the stairs and poked his head round the living-room door to say goodbye.

Back in the car, he headed for Gilbert Fortescue's home, though if his wife wore

Vixen he could think of no good reason for her to kill Keith Sutherland or Carol Mumford.

He drew a blank on the perfume with both the Fortescues and the Hurleys. By now, that left only the Sutherlands themselves. It was a short journey to their family home. Mary Sutherland opened the door.

She looked startled to see him. 'Back again? What do you want, Inspector?'

'Just a few more questions, Mrs Sutherland. It won't take long.'

With a faint sigh, she let him in and led him into the living room. There was no sign of Susie.

'Your daughter out?' he asked.

'Yes. She has several appointments today with potential clients.'

'So, how are you bearing up, Mrs Sutherland?' he asked. 'It must be a great comfort to you to have your daughter staying.'

'Yes. She might stay on here indefinitely actually and rent out her flat. It would keep her costs down while she gets her business off the ground. It makes sense. The house is way too big for me to rattle around in on my own.'

'Maybe you should sell it and get yourself an easy-to-manage flat?'

'Oh no. I couldn't do that. This is the family home. I want to keep it so that Susie and Ian can come back anytime they want. It's their inheritance. If I sold it and bought a flat the money would be sure to just dribble away. But you're not interested in my family concerns, I'm sure. You said you wanted to ask me some questions.'

'Yes.' Rafferty was damned if he knew what to ask her, but he managed to dredge up a couple of points. As he had with Derek Fowler, he asked if she had known that Ian's business was on the downward spiral.

To his surprise, she admitted it. 'It was too bad I couldn't help him. He just needed a little financial support until this recession is over. His father—' She broke off.

'You were going to say something about Mr Sutherland,' he prompted.

'Only that Keith's business was also going through a bad patch, so he was unable to help Ian.'

'Would he have helped him if he could?'

'Yes, I'm sure he would. Ian was his only son after all.'

Only son and only rival, was another way of looking at it.

'At least, with his share of the life insurance, he'll be able to prop the business up. It's a lifeline for him.'

A very fortunate and timely lifeline, was Rafferty's thought as he began to question his doubts about Ian Sutherland's guilt.

Though, of course, with Ian in prison, his business was likely to go to the wall anyway. And if he was convicted of his father's murder, he wouldn't receive the money anyway, as you couldn't profit from your own crime.

A silence fell – Rafferty had run out of things to ask.

'Was there anything else, Inspector?'

'No. That's it. Just tying up a few loose ends.' He didn't tell her that he was wracked with doubts over her son's guilt. What was the point in getting her hopes up if he failed to find someone else at whom he could point the finger?

'Could I use your bathroom, do you think, Mrs Sutherland?' He made the same excuse of drinking several mugs of tea at the station.

She nodded and told him where to find the toilet. Unfortunately, being a big house, it had a lavatory on the ground floor as well as upstairs. But he took a chance and crept up the stairs.

In the upstairs bathroom, he hit jackpot. A bottle of Vixen stood on the bathroom shelf – though whether it was Mary Sutherland's or one Susie had brought from her flat was a moot point, her things being jumbled up with her mother's on the bathroom shelf.

But it was a definite pointer to the possible

guilt of one of the women. Now, if he could only find something else...

Superintendent Bradley was waiting for him when he got back to his office.

'Where have you been, Rafferty?' he demanded. 'I've been asking for you for the last hour. You had your mobile switched off, too.'

Unwilling to reveal that he was still investigating other suspects in the case when Bradley thought he had the case – and Ian Sutherland's guilt – all sewn up, Rafferty came up with a more acceptable story. 'Sorry, sir. I was seeing one of my snouts. He gets a bit edgy if we're disturbed.'

'Seeing a snout, was it? What about?'

'About the spate of recent burglaries, sir,' Rafferty improvised. 'I thought he might give me a handle on them.'

'And did he?'

'Nothing concrete as yet, sir, but I'm working on him. He's proving a bit coy.'

'Hmm. Well don't go disappearing another time.'

'No, sir.'

'And leave your mobile switched on. I needed to contact you urgently. There's a press conference organized for this lunchtime about these burglaries. I want you there. One o'clock. Don't be late.' Bradley

274

banged out.

'He hasn't been hanging about in here for the last hour, has he?' he asked Llewellyn.

'No. He kept popping back.'

'What did you tell him?'

'What you told me to tell him.'

'That's good. It's as well for our stories to tally. Did he believe you?'

'I don't know. But it's fortunate that he can't prove it either way, isn't it?'

Rafferty grinned. 'Isn't it, though?' He told Llewellyn what he'd found in the Sutherlands' bathroom.

'Interesting,' he said. 'You think it could be significant?'

'Yes. Sanjay Gupta was positive that Vixen was the perfume he smelt. I think the trail's narrowing, Daff. It's got to be one of the Sutherland women. Susie must be favourite as I can't imagine a mother letting her son go to jail for something she did, whereas I don't think there's that much love lost between Susie and her brother.'

'You could be right.'

'I know I am.'

He knuckled down to the official work after that, spending what remained of the morning arranging for the usual suspects to be questioned over the burglaries.

Just before one, he paid a visit to the gents' and made ready for the press conference. It would probably mostly be the local press and TV, which was a relief. He hated press conferences and usually did his best to get out of them. Not trying to wriggle out of this one had been a sop to the belligerent Bradley. It wouldn't do to antagonize him over something else, especially when, if he was to have any chance of solving these crimes, he was likely to need to do his disappearing act again.

NINETEEN

The press conference came to an end over an hour later. Rafferty made his way back to his office, where Llewellyn was still beavering away.

'Anything new come in?' Rafferty asked as he sat down at his desk.

'Nothing much, though a couple of the burglary suspects were unable to give alibis as to where they were on the nights the burglaries took place.'

'Might get a result, then. Two results, if it gets Bradley off my back.'

'Lizzie Green and Tim Smales are bringing them in for questioning.' He glanced at the clock. 'They should be here soon. Lizzie rang in ten minutes ago.'

Lizzie rang from the custody suite a couple of minutes later and Rafferty and Llewellyn went down to question the two burglary suspects. Both were well known to them, being habitual offenders.

The first, Harry Crew, was brought into the interview room first. As expected, he denied everything.

'Trying to stitch me up again, Mr Rafferty?' he asked. 'I was home with my old lady on the nights you mentioned. I've just remembered.'

'What a memory you must have. Now me, I can't remember what I've done from one day to the next. Getting quite the homebody, then, aren't you? That's not like you, Harry.'

'Yes, well. I'm not as young as I was. Besides, I'm pretty well retired now, you know. There's too many places with the good stuff with security these days. When I was working, I liked a simple in and out, as you know, Mr Rafferty. It's all getting too complicated these days.'

Harry Crew wasn't noted for his proficiency in disabling security systems, so, against his better judgement, Rafferty was inclined to believe him. He let Crew go: he could always pick him up again if necessary.

The other suspect was a different case. Jimmy 'the Crack' Jameson was a noted safe man and several of the properties that had been burgled had had their safes cleaned out. Jimmy didn't have a wife and was a loner, so had been able to supply no ready alibi. Within half an hour, Rafferty had charged and bailed him.

'Right,' he said, as he and Llewellyn left the custody suite. 'That's that sorted. I'm off out again.'

'And what am I supposed to tell Super-intendent Bradley this time if he comes looking for you? Not another meeting with a snout?'

'No, I think not. Even Bradley wouldn't fall for the same excuse twice. Tell him I've gone to lunch. Even I'm entitled to a lunch break.'

'Where are you going?'

'Not to lunch, anyway. Though I can bring you a sandwich back if you like.'

'No, it's OK. I'll get something from the canteen.'

'Suit yourself. I don't suppose I'll be much more than an hour. Hold the fort. I'll tell you all about it when I get back.'

'And will you tell Bradley all about it, too?'

'Not a chance. Not yet, anyway.' Rafferty went out and drove to the Sutherlands' home.

'You again, Inspector,' said Susie, who answered the door. 'My mother told me you were here earlier.'

'Just call me a bad penny,' Rafferty told her. 'I'll keep turning up until I'm satisfied I've got the truth.'

'The truth? Are you sure you'd recognize it? After all, you arrested my poor, foolish brother. He's the last person to kill anyone, most of all my father. He was scared of him.'

'Perhaps that's a reason for killing him?'

'Never. You don't know Ian or you wouldn't say that.'

'Anyway, can I come in? I've got something I want to say to you both.'

'Why not?' She stood back.

Once again seated in the living room, Rafferty got straight to the point. 'I've begun having doubts about Ian's guilt,' he told them. It was the second time he'd made the confession, but Mary Sutherland acted as if he'd never said anything about it before.

She gasped, then said, 'Thank God. I thought—'

'I told you he didn't do it,' was Susie's blunt response.

'Yes, you did, didn't you? The thing is, I won't be able to release Ian until I find the real killer. Can either of you help me do that?'

'And how are we supposed to do that?' Susie asked with a hint of scorn. 'All we know is that he didn't do it. We have no idea who did.'

'Are you sure? What about you, Mrs Sutherland? Have you any idea who killed your husband?'

'No ... I ... that is ... No. No, I haven't.'

'You don't seem very sure. I think this was a very personal murder. Committed by someone who knew him well. Someone who knew he was likely to gatecrash his son's stag do. Not too many people would know where Ian was likely to be that evening. A handful, I should think.'

'I'm afraid we can't help you, Inspector,' said Susie. 'If there's nothing else?'

Reluctantly, Rafferty rose. If he'd been hoping for a confession from one of them he'd been disappointed. But it was worth a try. Susie struck him as hard-headed – she'd given most of the responses while her mother had barely said a word. Yet if she was hoping for her brother to carry the can for her killing of her father she seemed remarkably persistent in insisting he hadn't done it. A double bluff? Or simply a loving and innocent girl defending her brother?

He was back in the office in less than the hour he'd promised Llewellyn. 'Bradley show his face again?' he asked.

'No. He went out not five minutes after you. I went and questioned his secretary and she doesn't expect him back for the rest of the day.'

'Good.' Rafferty sat down and propped his feet on the desk. He told Llewellyn about his visit to the Sutherlands.

'What? Did you expect to get a confession from one of them?'

'You never know. I'm becoming more and more convinced that one of them killed Sutherland and Mumford. All I need is the proof. Any idea how I get it?'

Llewellyn shook his head.

'Neither have I. Maybe I'll have to try a bit of subterfuge?'

'What are you going to do? Bug the place?'

'It might come to that, but not just yet. I'm still hopeful that a guilty conscience will prompt one of them to confess. I can't see them leaving Ian to stew for something one of them did. It's only a matter of time.'

'Let's hope so,' said Llewellyn. 'Tea?'

'Please. And get me a sandwich, would you? I forgot to get one. Whatever the canteen's got left.'

While Llewellyn got the tea, Rafferty sat and stared out the window. A squall was blowing up. Rain lashed the windows and looked set to continue doing so for the rest of the day. Just as well he had no more visits

281

planned as he'd left his mac at home and still hadn't bought a replacement umbrella.

Llewellyn came back with the tea. 'They only had a salad sandwich left in the canteen.'

Rafferty pulled a face, but he took the sandwich anyway, unwrapped it and began to eat, pausing only to sip the hot tea. 'Reckon if I keep visiting the Sutherlands, they'll crack?'

'Or report you for harassment. Then Superintendent Bradley will know you're still pursuing the investigation.'

'Last thing I want.'

'Why are you so sure Ian Sutherland's innocent?'

'I'm not sure. But I do feel I was – what did you call it? Prec–prec?'

'Precipitate?'

'Yeah, that. But I had Bradley pushing me for a result and Sutherland seemed a gift, you know. Right on the spot and with a reason – several reasons – to want his dad dead.'

Llewellyn nodded.

'I should have held off, I see that now. I should have argued with Bradley when he insisted I charged Sutherland. All I've succeeded in doing is making my job harder. Bradley'll never listen if I go to him now and say I don't think Sutherland's guilty after all. He's already had his head patted by Region. All he'll want me to do is concentrate on making the charges stick.' He sighed. 'Why does life have to be such a bitch? And don't say I brought it on myself.'

'I wasn't going to. You seemed to have persuaded yourself of that without my help.'

Rafferty stared challengingly at him for a moment, then let it go. He finished his sandwich and sighed again. 'I suppose I'll have to go through the motions with Sutherland, show willing and all that.'

'But meanwhile?'

'Meanwhile, the investigation goes on. It'll leave a nasty taste if Sutherland's convicted. Not to mention ruining my track record.'

There were still witness statements trickling in on Sutherland's and Mumford's murders. Rafferty read his way through them, but there was nothing of interest, nor likely to be now. He handed them to Llewellyn.

What to do now? he wondered. It seemed a pity to lose the rest of the day when he could be doing something on the murder case, especially when Bradley was safely out of the way and unlikely to be on his tail. He glanced out of the window. It was still chucking it down. He was reluctant to leave the office and go out in it, but he hauled himself to his feet anyway.

'Going out again?'

'Seems a shame to waste time while Bradley's out of the way. Come with me if you like – unless you're worried you'll blot your copybook.'

'Perhaps, like you, I'm more concerned with blotting the annals of justice on this case.' Llewellyn pulled on his mac – unlike Rafferty, he'd obviously listened to the weather forecast before leaving home that morning.

'Good man. Let's go.'

'Where are we going, anyway?'

'We're going on the knocker. I thought we might question the people who live opposite The Railway Arms.'

'But they'll have been questioned once already. What do you hope to achieve?'

'God knows. Something. Anything. It's better than sitting in the station twiddling my thumbs.'

Rafferty drove. In spite of the traffic, which the rain had brought out, the journey didn't take more than a few minutes. He parked in the yard of The Railway Arms, got out of the car and looked around him, recalling the night of Keith Sutherland's murder and how spooked it had made him feel as he had stood alone waiting for the cavalry to arrive. Ridiculous, really, looking back on it, but at the time the uneasiness had been real enough. Perhaps he'd sensed the aura of evil?

'Come on,' he said to Llewellyn as he shrugged the feeling aside and headed across the road.

The first door he knocked at brought no response. Of course, at this time of day most people would be at work. He tried the next door. This time they struck luckier in that a woman answered the door. Not that she was any help.

'We sit in the back room, see?' she told them. 'It's quieter.'

The next door was another no response. It wasn't till they got to the last house in the row that their luck changed. An elderly man answered. He was taciturn at first, disinclined to answer their questions, but he thawed and invited them in when Rafferty mentioned that he was a friend of Andy Strong, the landlord of The Railway Arms.

'Good bloke, Andy,' said Cyril Matlock as he bid them be seated in his front living room. 'Always got time for an old man, not like some pub landlords. Doesn't moan, either, when I sit nursing a half of mild all evening.' He sat down on a hard chair, rasped his hand across his whiskery chin and asked how he could help them.

'It's about the night of the murder, Mr Matlock. The one that occurred in the pub yard.'

'I've already been asked about that. I had two of your blokes knocking on my door the morning after. Awful thing to happen to Andy Strong. He runs a tidy pub. Mind, I know for a fact his trade's increased. Usual ghouls coming to see where it happened, I suppose. See if they can spot any blood-stains.' He shook his wispy-haired head at the modern world. 'I was sitting in here all that evening, listening to the radio and watching out for passing yobboes. Some of them like to pee in my front garden, you know. I nearly caught one once, but I can't move so quickly now with the arthritis, and he got away.'

'About the night of the murder, Mr Matlock,' Rafferty tried again. 'Did you notice anyone going into the car park pretty late on in the evening?'

'I saw a gang of yobs. Probably seeing what they could steal, but they left well before the stabbing. I saw a few other people, as well, later on, but they were older and all in twos or threes and that was before I saw Keith Sutherland staggering out of the pub and round to the car park. A bunch of lads came out just after him but they headed on into town. One of them was his son, Ian, I think.'

Rafferty glanced at Llewellyn. Here was

justification for his doubts about Ian Sutherland's guilt. 'You're sure all the five lads headed into town, sir?' he questioned quietly.

'Sure I'm sure. They were shouting and carrying on. I was in two minds about going out and telling them to put a sock in it.'

'You knew Keith Sutherland and his son?'

'Yes. It's my local. I know all the regulars and Keith for one was more regular than most, if you get my drift.'

Rafferty was beginning to get excited. He tried to control it. 'Tell me, Mr Matlock – did you see anyone leave the car park after Keith Sutherland had entered it?'

Mr Matlock nodded. 'Yeah. Saw a woman, didn't I? On a bike. But it couldn't have been her that killed him.'

'Why not?'

'Knifing's not a woman's crime. And Keith was a big man, not easy to attack.'

Easy enough, thought Rafferty, if he was half-cut and had his back to the assailant. Of course, they hadn't released to the media the fact that he had been stabbed in the back. It was always as well to keep something back. 'Can you describe this woman? Can you describe her bike?'

'Reckon I could. Is there a reward?'

'No reward beyond doing your civic duty.' God, he thought, how pompous did that sound?'

Cyril Matlock snorted at this. 'Keith Sutherland's no great loss to the world. Argumentative sort.'

'The woman, sir,' Rafferty reminded him.

'All right, all right. I didn't see her face. She had a scarf well over most of it and had her head down.'

'Would you say she was young or old? Fat or thin?'

'Middle-aged would be my guess. And she was a bit on the dumpy side. Mind, she fairly raced out of the yard for an old 'un.' He pierced them with a suddenly much sharper gaze. 'Why? Do you reckon she was the one who done it?'

Rafferty nodded. 'I reckon she might be, at that.' He paused, then asked, 'And what about the bike? Could you see the colour?'

'Yes. The bike's easy. It was white. A woman's bike. It had a wicker basket on the front.'

Rafferty beamed. 'Thank you, sir. You've been a great help. Tell me, how come you didn't tell any of this to the officers who spoke to you before?'

'They didn't ask me. And as I said, I didn't think you'd be looking for a woman.'

Rafferty's beam faded. All these days, all the man hours wasted when the case could have been solved days ago. Someone was going to get a roasting when he got back to the station. 'Can you come back with us and give a formal statement?' he asked now. 'Just for the record.' And to have something concrete to show to Bradley when he was ready to break the news about Ian Sutherland's innocence.

'Certainly. As long as someone drives me back as I can't walk far.'

'Of course.'

'I'll get my mac.'

Rafferty and Llewellyn had to curtail their excitement. Rafferty didn't send for a constable to take the statement when they got back to the station. This was one statement he wanted to take himself. It didn't take long. Rafferty whisked up a car to take Mr Matlock back home, then they hurried up to their office.

'Looks like I was half right and our killer is Mary Sutherland, rather than Susie,' Rafferty said, a hint of triumph in his voice as his beliefs were vindicated. 'How the hell did we miss her and that bike on the CCTV?'

'I suppose because we were looking for a car. It's not a common occurrence for someone intent on murder to use a pushbike as their getaway vehicle of choice.'

'No, I suppose not.' He frowned as his triumph faded. 'But it's still not proof. One old man probably with defective eyesight doesn't make for a strong case against her.'

'Then it's up to us to find something more.'

Rafferty nodded. He wished he knew what that something more might be...

TWENTY

Rafferty decided to suppress Cyril Matlock's statement for the time being. He was convinced that Ian Sutherland being incarcerated was the only thing that would persuade Mary Sutherland to confess. If Ian were released she would never admit the truth. He supposed it was unfair on Ian, but he had reason to hope that young man wouldn't be behind bars for much longer.

It wasn't easy to persuade Llewellyn of the advantages of suppressing evidence.

'But don't you see,' Rafferty argued. 'This gives us our one chance to nail her. Do you really think she'll let her son be sentenced for murder? I don't. I think it's just a case of out-waiting her conscience.'

'It might be a long wait. She's shown no sign of telling the truth so far.'

'That's why I've been applying pressure. She'll crack, I'm sure of it.'

'I hope you're right. Only don't forget you're making me complicit in the suppression.'

'Does that mean you'll do it?'

'Yes, but under protest.'

'Don't worry. If Bradley finds out I'll take the blame. As far as you're concerned, you were just obeying orders.'

'I wish I could believe the superintendent will see it like that.'

'Why do you think I didn't date the statement? I can produce it any time I like and put my date of choice on it.'

Llewellyn still looked dubious, but at least, for now, he was going along with it. And Rafferty thought it might well be possible to square away Cyril Matlock about the date he'd given the statement, even if he had to find a small reward from his own pocket.

All in all, it had been quite a productive day and Rafferty was well pleased at the end of it.

Llewellyn was still subdued and Rafferty tried to jolly him up a bit. 'It's in a good cause, Dafyd, the interests of truth.'

'I'd feel happier about that if we didn't have to first suppress the truth.'

'So would I, but the ends justify the means in this case, I'm sure of it.'

Llewellyn still didn't look convinced and Rafferty decided to leave well enough alone. He'd got Llewellyn's agreement to suppress Matlock's statement; he'd have to be content with that. He headed home, running through the continuing rain to his car.

When Rafferty reached home and told Abra what he'd done, she was inclined to take Llewellyn's side.

'But don't you see,' he said. 'This is the only way to get the truth.'

'Maybe so. But I can't help thinking of that poor boy languishing in jail for something he didn't do.'

Rafferty filled the kettle and banged it down on its base. 'Not you as well? All of a sudden, I seem to be surrounded by bleeding-heart liberals.'

'It's hardly liberal to want to free an innocent man.'

'He's an estate agent, for God's sake. I don't suppose he's as innocent as all that.'

'Now you're being facetious.'

'Am I? Am I really?' Rafferty wasn't too sure what the word meant, but the tone of voice told him all he needed to know. He didn't want to argue. He made the tea and brought the mugs into the living room. 'It should only be for a few days,' he placated, unhappy that he seemed to have got on

Abra's wrong side all over again. Unwilling for the bad feeling between them to fester, he said, 'If I haven't had him released in a few days you can go and see Superintendent Bradley yourself and tell him what Cyril Matlock said. I can't say fairer than that.'

'Yes you could, Joe. You could say a lot fairer.'

Fortunately, she let the matter drop and sipped her tea. 'So you're hoping for a confession?' she questioned.

Rafferty nodded. 'I think a confession's the only way I'll prove who did it. I reckon it's only a matter of time before I get one.' That was what he hoped, anyway.

But no confession had been forthcoming by the next morning. And Llewellyn was no happier at their deceit today than he had been the previous day and as the minutes and hours ticked away he grew even less so.

'How long are you going to keep this up?' Llewellyn asked. 'Days? Weeks? Months?'

As long as it takes, was Rafferty's thought, but he said, 'I told you – just a few days. I can't see it being longer than that.'

Llewellyn looked at him, but said nothing more.

After that, they both settled down to work. But the silence in the office wasn't a comfortable one and, pretty soon, Rafferty found an excuse to take himself off.

He drove aimlessly, or thought he did, but pretty soon he found himself parked up outside the Sutherlands' home. He sat, tapping the steering wheel, sending thought-waves to Mary Sutherland to come out and admit her guilt. However, the front door stayed firmly closed and after half an hour, knowing he couldn't ride around aimlessly for the rest of the day – Bradley would be sure to ask where he was and in his current mood, Llewellyn might admit he had no idea, which would go down like a bacon buttie at a Bar Mitzvah – he drove back to the station and Llewellyn's disapproval.

He parked up in the station yard and remained where he was for a few minutes, reluctant to go back to his office. But eventually, he climbed out and went inside.

Llewellyn didn't look up when he opened the office door.

'There's no need to sulk,' Rafferty told him peevishly.

'I'm not sulking. I was concentrating.'

'What on? There can be precious-little new information coming in.'

Llewellyn's silence conceded that this was so. Indeed, he didn't hand the latest paperwork that he was so assiduously studying to Rafferty to read.

Rafferty, put in the wrong by Abra,

Llewellyn and his conscience, burst out, 'OK. Have you got a better idea?'

'I have, as it happens. If you're so convinced of Mrs Sutherland's guilt, I think we should challenge her. Tell her honestly that we believe she killed her husband.'

'And you think she'll admit it? Just like that?'

'Why not? It's what you believe will happen by virtue of holding her son in custody.'

As that was true, Rafferty could produce no argument to gainsay Llewellyn's claim. 'I'm not ready to do that yet,' Rafferty told him. 'Before I challenge her, I want some more evidence.'

'Like what? What more evidence do you think we're going to get this far along in the investigation?'

Rafferty didn't know, but he was unwilling to say so. When he didn't answer, another silence, as uncomfortable as before, descended.

At least Bradley didn't trouble him, being satisfied that they had the murderer safely under lock and key. It was the only bright spot in a difficult day.

The morning finally dragged its way to lunchtime and it was with relief that Rafferty took himself off to the canteen.

Tom Kendall was ahead of him in the lunch queue and as they sat down at a table together, Rafferty asked him how his warehouse theft case was going. 'Chummy coughed up any more of his customers' names?'

Kendall shook his head. 'Reckons he can't remember any more. Still, we've got a nice haul. I'm satisfied. I hear congratulations are in order for you, too.'

Rafferty gave what felt like a sickly smile.

'I must say, you don't look too happy about it,' Kendall commented. 'What's the matter? Having belated doubts about your suspect's guilt?'

As that was exactly what Rafferty was having and with good reason, he was hard-pressed to deny it. But in the interests of self-preservation, he managed it. He didn't know how convinced Tom Kendall was by his answer but his sceptical grin spoke volumes. 'You'd better stay away from Bradley,' was his advice.

If only Bradley could be relied upon to stay away from *him*.

The long, depressing day finally wound to a close. Rafferty wished he could recapture the optimism he had felt the previous day. But it was as far away as if it had never been. He was beginning to believe Llewellyn was right and he should think about accusing Mary Sutherland and seeing if she admitted her guilt. The only trouble was he'd have shown his hand and if she made no admission where would that leave him?

He still couldn't understand why she hadn't come forward and told the truth. Was she really prepared for her son to go down for a crime she had committed? Always supposing she *was* guilty and he wasn't making altogether too much of Cyril Matlock's evidence.

Round and round his thoughts went, now convinced of Mary Sutherland's guilt, next full of doubts that he was on the wrong track altogether. By the time he packed up for the day and went home, he was more confused than he remembered being in any investigation before.

But there was one thing he could do. He didn't know if it would go further towards proving Mary Sutherland's guilt, but he wanted to be sure everything had been covered as thoroughly as it could be.

TWENTY-ONE

Rafferty woke up with the most awful head-ache thumping between his eyes. And when he tried to move, his limbs, too, ached all over. He went hot, then cold and he laid his head back down on the pillows with a groan.

'What's the matter? You look awful.' Abra leaned over on an elbow and laid a hand on his forehead. 'You're burning up.'

'I think I've got the flu. My entire body aches.'

'Poor you. Sure it's not just a bad cold? You men always tend to promote your illnesses above their station.'

'Not this time. This is much worse than a cold. You'll have to ring the station. I can't go in like this. I'll speak to Llewellyn later, let him know what I want him and the rest of the team to concentrate on.'

Abra edged out of bed. 'I'll get you some painkillers and a hot drink. Could you eat something?'

'No. I've got no appetite and my mouth

tastes funny. All metallic. Maybe if I clean my teeth it'll taste better.'

'You do that while I put the kettle on. I won't be long.'

Ten minutes later, Rafferty was settled back against the pillows feeling a little better for the painkillers and tea. At least his headache had receded to a dull roar.

Abra bustled in with a flask. 'I've made you up some coffee. It should see you through the day.' She put her hand in her pocket and pulled out a packet of tablets. 'And here's some more painkillers. Sure I can't get you something to eat before I go to work?'

Rafferty shook his head. 'No. I've no appetite. I might get myself something later if I feel hungry.'

'OK. I won't kiss you. I don't want to catch the dreaded lurgy. I'll see you later.'

'OK, sweetheart.'

Rafferty dozed for a while and took some more painkillers with his coffee. He felt restless; the bedcovers seemed too heavy, the pillows too hard, the light through the windows too bright. He threw the bedcovers back and then immediately felt cold again. He put on his dressing gown and padded along the hall to the living room. Maybe a hot toddy would help? He poured a large measure of Jameson's into a glass and brought it into the kitchen. While he waited for the kettle to boil, he rang Llewellyn. Abra had earlier contacted Bill Beard, the duty officer, and he'd passed on Rafferty's message.

'How are you feeling?' Llewellyn asked.

'Terrible. I'd have tried to come in but I'd be worse than useless. Anything new happened?'

'No, but Superintendent Bradley's been in asking after you.'

Rafferty gave a wry laugh. 'Exuding concern and sympathy, I don't doubt, when he learned about my bed of pain.'

'Something like that. Why? Did you expect him to rush out and buy a get well card?'

'A get well or get sacked card is more Bradley's line. Hopefully, I'll be back at work in a few days. And at least, in the interim, I'll have plenty of time to think about the case without Bradley raining on my parade. Meanwhile, if you can continue with the review of the murders in between the other cases. I'm sorry to land this on you, Dafyd, but as I said, I hope to be back in a few days.'

'You just concentrate on getting well and leave the rest to me. I can farm out the other cases to the rest of the team and concentrate on the Sutherland and Mumford investigations.'

'Has Bradley suggested appointing another inspector to take over the case?'

'Not so far. I presume he's hanging fire to see if you're off for more than a few days. If you are, he'll probably review it.'

'I don't want that to happen. This is *my* investigation, no one else's. I'll drag myself from my bed of pain if necessary to prevent someone else taking over the case. Anyway, I just wanted to speak to you and make sure you're still on it. I'll get off the phone now and let you get on with it. I wish I didn't feel so rough, but there's no oddsing it. I'll be better when I'm better.'

'Then I'll see you when I see you. Keep taking the tablets.'

Rafferty smiled as he replaced the receiver. Keep taking the tablets, said Llewellyn. He'd taken six already. He supposed he ought to go steady or he'd have an overdose to add to his troubles.

He made his hot toddy and took it back to bed. He dozed again after he'd drunk it, images of the investigation floating past his mind. So, he thought, if Ian Sutherland hadn't killed his father and Carol Mumford, who had? For the moment, he put aside all thoughts of Mary Sutherland as the guilty party and concentrated on the other suspects. There weren't that many serious contenders. Derek Fowler, for instance, if he

301

could break his Cambridge alibi. He had the most to gain; the entirety of the ownership of SuperElect, a comfortable, leisurely retirement and money in the bank.

Had they tried hard enough to trace his possible return to Elmhurst? No one had seen much of him on the Thursday evening in his hotel. He hadn't eaten dinner there. Either he was on a strict diet or he'd eaten elsewhere. But they'd been unable to trace such a restaurant. When questioned, Fowler had said he'd felt unwell and had stayed in his room and skipped dinner. But Fowler looked a natural trencherman and seemed unlikely to skip a meal, particularly as it transpired that the hotel's restaurant had recently received a Michelin star for its cuisine. How to break his alibi was the question.

The next morning saw Rafferty sniffing and sneezing and feeling even more sorry for himself. He should be immune from flu at his age, he thought, indignantly. It wasn't fair that he should be laid low when he needed to be up and about and solving the case. He thought he already *had* solved it, but he had no way of proving it. Not unless he could extract a confession...

He spent the day much as he'd spent the previous one, alternately dosing himself up

302

with painkillers and hot toddies. He still had no appetite, but forced himself to eat some cereal for breakfast if only to stop him feeling light-headed.

Abra was home early and made him some scrambled eggs and toast, which he somehow forced down past his sore throat.

'Feeling any better?' she asked as she watched him eat.

Rafferty pulled a face. 'Not so's you'd notice. I think I'm dying. Maybe you should get the doctor in.'

'There's no need for that, Joe. Try to be a little more stoical. You're no worse than you were yesterday, are you?'

'I suppose not. But I'm no better, either. I told Llewellyn I'd be back at work in a few days, but I won't be if I don't start to improve soon.'

'You're too impatient. It has to run its course. And talking of Dafyd, he said he'd try to pop in this evening. I rang him from work to let him know how you are.'

'How's the case going? Did he say?'

'No. And I didn't ask him. You can worry about that when you're feeling better. The flu's giving you enough of a headache, I would think, without looking for more.'

She left him to his own devices then while she went to get her own evening meal.

Llewellyn arrived an hour later. The case

hadn't progressed any further: Ian Sutherland was still incarcerated and looked likely to remain so; nobody's alibi had been broken and no one had confessed. All in all, the day had gone about as well as Rafferty felt.

'When do you think you'll be back at work?' Llewellyn asked.

'It won't be tomorrow, anyway, not the way I feel. But I've been dosing myself up like a tame pharmacist, so I'm hopeful I'll be over the worst before too long. How's Bradley taking my continued absence?'

'I haven't seen him today. He's been at meetings for most of it. But if he was concerned he would have called me in to see him, so I wouldn't worry.'

'At least he doesn't seem set on replacing me on the case, which is something. I don't want that to happen, so keep looking busy, Daff, if he comes by the office.'

'I *am* busy. I don't need to put on a special show for the superintendent.'

'I know. But it's good for your promotion prospects. How's the studying going, anyway? All right?'

Llewellyn nodded. 'I'm putting in as many hours as I can and Maureen's testing me.'

'You'll be all right,' Rafferty reassured him. 'If I can pass the inspector's exams, you'll walk it. It'll be a doddle.' He changed the subject. 'How's the warehouse investigation going? Has Tom managed to get any more information from the perpetrators?'

'I don't know. I haven't seen him. Why are you so interested in the case?'

Rafferty tried for an unconcerned reply. 'I just like to know what's going on, that's all. Given that his case might yet prove to have a tie-in with ours.'

'I thought you'd given that idea up.'

'I have, more or less. But it doesn't do to discount possibilities too soon; something you should be aware of with inspector's exams looming.'

'I am aware of it,' Llewellyn assured him somewhat testily. 'I just don't want to waste time on a dead end, which is what I think that is.'

'You're probably right,' Rafferty was quick to agree, not wanting the Welshman to start probing and maybe find out his real interest in his colleague's case.

'I'll be getting off and let you rest,' Llewellyn said.

'OK. Thanks for popping by. I'll see you when I see you.'

Llewellyn left and Rafferty was free to dwell on what was happening at the station. At least Bradley didn't seem to be poking his nose in. Of course, he thought the case was already wrapped up and wasn't aware that Rafferty was still actively pursuing it. Or rather he would be if he wasn't so ill. And then Bradley probably trusted Llewellyn more than he did him to get the paperwork right. Rafferty wished he had some news on the progress of the warehouse case. But he couldn't worry about that now. It would only make his head ache even more without achieving anything.

No, it was the murder case he had to think about and before Abra came to bed he did just that.

It was another four days before Rafferty felt well enough to return to work. He found Superintendent Bradley in a testy mood and not at all inclined to show sympathy to his ailing subordinate.

'So you're back at last,' was how he greeted Rafferty when he put his head round the superintendent's door. 'About time. All those days off for nobbut a piddling cold.'

'I had flu, sir,' Rafferty defended himself.

'Flu? Pooh! Catch me taking all that time off for a few sniffles. Anyway, now you're back I want you to get on and try to produce a result on these burglaries. We're getting bad press on them and I want it to stop.'

Bad media attention was Bradley's bête noire. He much preferred to be a media darling.

'You'd best get along to your office and make a start now that you are here. There are going to be no relapses, I hope.'

'I hope not, too, sir.'

'Yes, well, off you go and don't start spreading any remaining germs about. I don't want more of my officers going on the sick list.'

'No, sir.' Three bags full, sir, he thought as he left Bradley's office and made for his own. Llewellyn was already there, of course, as usual.

'Morning, Daff,' said Rafferty. 'I've just come from a little pep talk with the super. It seems I'm under instruction not to sneeze over anyone, so if you see me about to let rip hand me a tissue quick.'

Llewellyn smiled. 'What am I? The designated team nurse? Just tell me you won't start calling me Florence.'

'Only if you start wearing a cap with streamers. So, what's new? Any advance on the burglaries case?'

'Yes. Jameson's admitted all the burglaries. I finished interviewing him ten minutes ago and as I said, he's admitted them all.'

'That's great. A good result. Well done, Daff. Has Bradley assigned us anything new?'

'He doesn't know we've got a result on the burglaries yet. No doubt he will as soon as he knows.'

The rest of the day passed relatively quietly. Even so, Rafferty was glad when it was over. He still found he felt tired at the least exertion. The flu had taken more out of him that he had realized. It would be a relief to get home and have Abra fuss over him.

However, Abra had other ideas. 'You'll have to get your own meal tonight, Joe,' she told him. 'I'm going out with the girls.'

'But you never said. I thought we'd have a quiet night in together.'

'You thought I'd wait on you hand and foot, you mean. And I would normally seeing as you're still recuperating. Just not tonight. And I did tell you. I told you last night and again this morning. You just weren't listening. There're plenty of frozen meals in the freezer. All you've got to do is pick one and put it in the microwave. I might be late. Don't wait up.' And with that, she gave him a quick kiss and was out the door.

Rafferty sighed. His lower lip drooped. Maybe when they were married Abra would take the 'in sickness and in health' bit more seriously. He'd looked forward to a bit of cosseting all day, especially after Bradley's less than sympathetic welcome back that morning.

Morosely, he poked about in the freezer

and selected a casserole with cheese dump-lings and stuck it in the microwave.

He cheered up a bit as he remembered there was football on the telly. Maybe the night wouldn't be such a washout after all. With footie, Jameson's and a casserole, the evening looked set as fair as it was likely to get.

Thirty minutes later, meal eaten, he set-tled down with a glass of Jameson's in front of the television, half wishing he hadn't been so quick to let his brother, Mickey, provide houseroom to the giant plasma TV. But it was too late now and perhaps it was for the best.

Four hours later he woke with a start, having missed the football entirely. Abra came in and seeing him sprawled on the settee, empty glass still precariously clasped in his hand, said, 'I see you're still self-medicating.'

'You look pretty well medicated yourself, my darling. Did you have a good time?'

'Great. I'm going to bed. Are you com-ing?'

Rafferty nodded and followed Abra to the bedroom. To his dismay, she was feeling frisky, but Rafferty pleaded continuing ill-health for his lack of manly fibre.

Abra wasn't amused and turned over in a huff when her overtures were rebuffed, leaving him to lay awake after his earlier snoozefest and contemplate his shortcomings.

'I've decided to have another look through the CCTV footage,' Rafferty said decisively as soon as he came in the following morning. 'I still feel there's likely to be something there to give some more proof to Mary Sutherland's guilt. I can't believe that, between her home and The Railway Arms, her and the bike don't show up somewhere.'

'Superintendent Bradley won't like you wasting your time on such routine work,' Llewellyn warned him.

'I won't tell him if you don't. Anyway, for the moment, I only want to check on the tapes for Sutherland's murder. If I get nothing from that I'll try those from the night of Carol Mumford's killing. What are we looking at? Half an hour's worth of footage? But I'm going to look at each second of it, with no skimming. I've just got a feeling about it, so don't try to dissuade me.'

'I wasn't going to,' said Llewellyn. 'I'll go and get the tea.'

'Good man. I'll need a hot, sweet brew to get me through it. I haven't sat through half an hour's worth of CCTV since I was Lilley's age and we didn't even have CCTV then.'

★ ★ ★

Rafferty's stint at staring goggle-eyed at the screen of CCTV footage covering the late evening of Keith Sutherland's death seemed to have borne some fruit, rather to his surprise.

He had already sat through twenty minutes of the tape for the night of the first murder, when he called Llewellyn into the viewing room.

He pointed to the right hand corner of the screen. 'Tell me what you think that is.'

Llewellyn peered over his shoulder. 'It looks like part of a bike tyre.'

'That's what I thought.' He switched the tape. 'Now take a look at that one.'

'A bike tyre again. White, same as the other one.'

'Right. And one is close to the Sutherlands' home and the other not far from The Railway Arms. Bit of a coincidence, don't you think? Whoever was riding it seems to have made sure to keep their face off any cameras. The two bikes look identical and—'

'I think you're rushing on a little. We don't know that it's the same bike.'

'No, but we know that two similar bikes were out and about in the vicinity of Mary Sutherland's home and the scene of the first murder. And we have Cyril Matlock's evidence of a white bike being at the scene as well to back this up. It's a start. It's a definite start. It's time to find out if one of our suspects owns a white bike, then we'll see.'

Llewellyn peered closer. 'Go in and get a close-up of that section.'

'You know I don't know how to do that,' Rafferty protested. 'You do it. Here, sit down.' Rafferty relinquished his chair.

Llewellyn sat down and with a few keystrokes had brought up two magnified sections of screen.

'Definitely the same bike,' said Rafferty. 'Shame you can't see a face. But it's not Ian Sutherland – he's too tall. It's a woman's bike, so that leaves us with Mary and Susie Sutherland. They both claimed they were home alone that night, so either could have gone out. I think it's favourite we get search warrants and see if we can't find that bike – it's pretty distinctive with the white trim, the dented tyre trim and its basket. Maybe we're nearer to solving this investigation than I thought we were. We've certainly got possible motives for both of them.'

Llewellyn quickly organized the two search warrants and the teams descended simultaneously. The white lady's bike with the dented fender and the basket was found in Mary Sutherland's garden shed.

Of course she protested her innocence. But Rafferty had got Llewellyn to print off the still pictures of the bike and its rider. Further magnification had revealed that the rider had worn a distinctive ring on the ring finger. It was large and ornate with a big diamond and surrounded by other stones that were possibly emeralds – the exact match of the one worn by Mary Sutherland.

'We know it was you, Mrs Sutherland,' said Rafferty. He tapped the two photos. 'Here's our proof. So why did you do it? For the money? For revenge for his infidelity? To make sure your two children had the money – the one for her new business and the other for his wedding? All of the above?'

To his surprise, she capitulated.

'All of the above and none of them. I was lonely, you see. So lonely. Keith was always out, either at work, courting work or courting women. I was tired of the humiliation of the last. He wasn't even any company when he *was* home. We never talked. *He* never talked. I knew if he were dead, and dead before he hit seventy and his term insurance was null and void, we'd all benefit. I knew I was in with a chance that Susie would move back home, at least while she got her new business up and running, to save cash. You could, I suppose, say I killed for company.'

She smiled suddenly. It was quite chilling and Rafferty felt his flesh shudder against his spine.

'Now Susie will come home. Maybe Ian too and we can be one big happy family again.'

Strange, Rafferty thought, that it didn't seem to occur to her that even if Susie and Ian *did* come home, she wouldn't be there to greet them. Still, she'd have plenty of company in prison.

'And what about Carol Mumford?' he asked. 'I presume you killed her, too?'

She nodded. 'You suppose right. I thought it only fitting that if she relished my husband's company so much in life she could have it in death, too. They deserved each other. Now I can have some peace. A rest from all the hate.'

TWENTY-TWO

Rafferty and Abra were throwing a reconciliation party. It had been Rafferty's idea – to prove to Abra that he wasn't the Scrooge he felt he'd appeared over the wedding arrangements. He hadn't stinted on the drink or the food: he'd even hired a DJ and the reception room of one of the local pubs for the occasion.

He had a surprise for Abra. He'd decided this was to be no half-hearted reconciliation on his part. Abra had been keen before their break-up that they sell both their flats and buy a house. Rafferty hadn't been nearly so keen, but now, he'd changed his mind. And with the current investigations both concluded, he'd had the spare time to go round the local estate agents and get house particulars.

He'd found half a dozen that would suit. He'd wrapped the particulars up in a pretty parcel tied with a red ribbon – or rather, he'd got his ma to do it so it wasn't his usual ham-fisted effort. He'd even ordered a cake in the shape of a man and a woman kissing. That had been a hit with Abra. By the time he handed her the parcel, she was quite starry-eyed.

'What's this?' she asked. 'A present as well as a party? You have turned over a new leaf.'

'When I turn over a new leaf, I do it thoroughly, sweetpea. Open your present.'

Abra did so. 'What's this? Pictures of houses? Why?'

'Because I want you to choose one. Take your pick. I'm easy. The choice is yours, my little apple strudel.'

'Oh Joe. You mean it? Really?'

'Really. We can go and look at the ones you want to see over the next weekend. Call it my re-engagement gift. No more Mr Tight-wad, I promise.'

'Don't go making promises you can't keep, Joe.' She smiled. 'Don't worry. I won't keep you to any of the more expensive ones. I, too, have learned my lesson.' To prove it, she kissed him. She made to tear the estate agents' particulars in half, but then paused and grinned. 'Only joking. I'll keep you to this promise.'

COA